the
MUTTS™
diaries

Other Books by Patrick McDonnell

Mutts
Cats and Dogs: Mutts II
More Shtuff: Mutts III
Yesh!: Mutts IV
Our Mutts: Five
A Little Look-See: Mutts VI
What Now: Mutts VII
I Want to Be the Kitty: Mutts VIII
Dog-Eared: Mutts IX
Who Let the Cat Out: Mutts X
Everyday Mutts
Animal Friendly
Call of the Wild
Stop and Smell the Roses
Earl & Mooch
Our Little Kat King
Bonk!
A Shtinky Little Christmas
Cat Crazy

˙ö˙

Mutts Sundays
Sunday Mornings
Sunday Afternoons
Sunday Evenings
Best of Mutts

˙ö˙

Shelter Stories

the MUTTS™
diaries

 PATRICK M^cDONNELL •

Andrews McMeel
Publishing
Kansas City • Sydney • London

Mooch's Diary

·EARL and MOOCH·
I'M A DOG.
HE'S A CAT.
YET, WE UNDERSTAND EACH OTHER COMPLETELY!
WHAT ARE YOU TALKING ABOUT!?!

CRASH
OOPS.

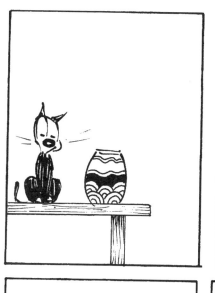

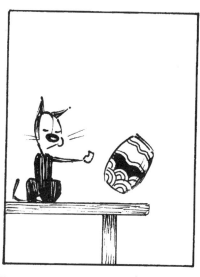

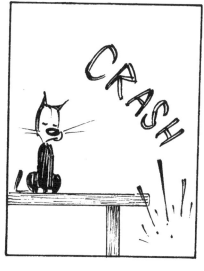

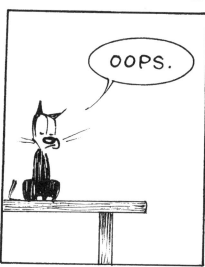

OKAY! EVERYTHING OFF THE TABLE!
HEY! NOT EVERY-THING!!!

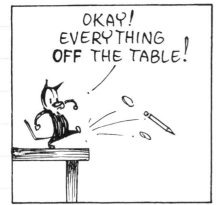

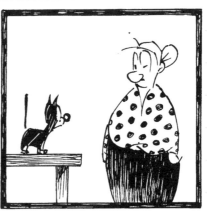

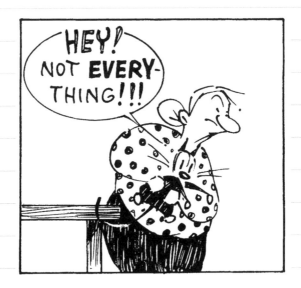

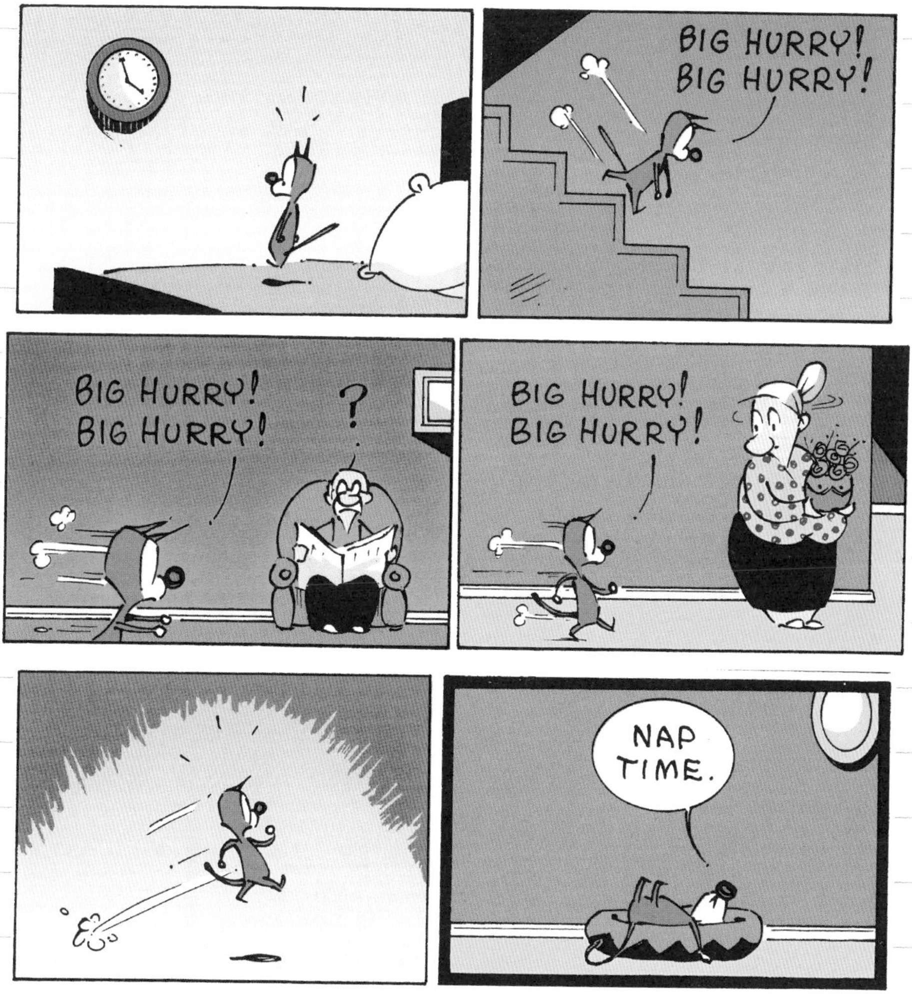
BIG HURRY!
BIG HURRY!
BIG HURRY!
BIG HURRY!
?
BIG HURRY!
BIG HURRY!
NAP
TIME.

MOOCHIE!
WHY WON'T YOU COME DOWN FOR DINNER?
WHY WON'T SHE COME UP?

SQUEEK
SQUEEK
SQUEEK
IF YOU SHQUEAK IT — HE WILL COME.

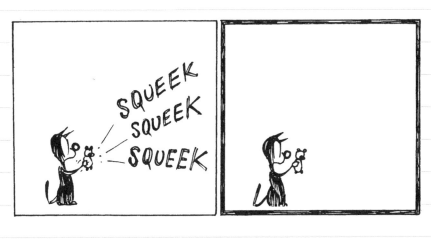

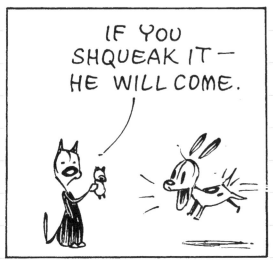

EARL, CAN YOU TELL ME WHAT DATE IT IS?
MARCH FIRST.
O.K.
HUP
HUP
THERE NOW...
WHAT DATE IS IT?

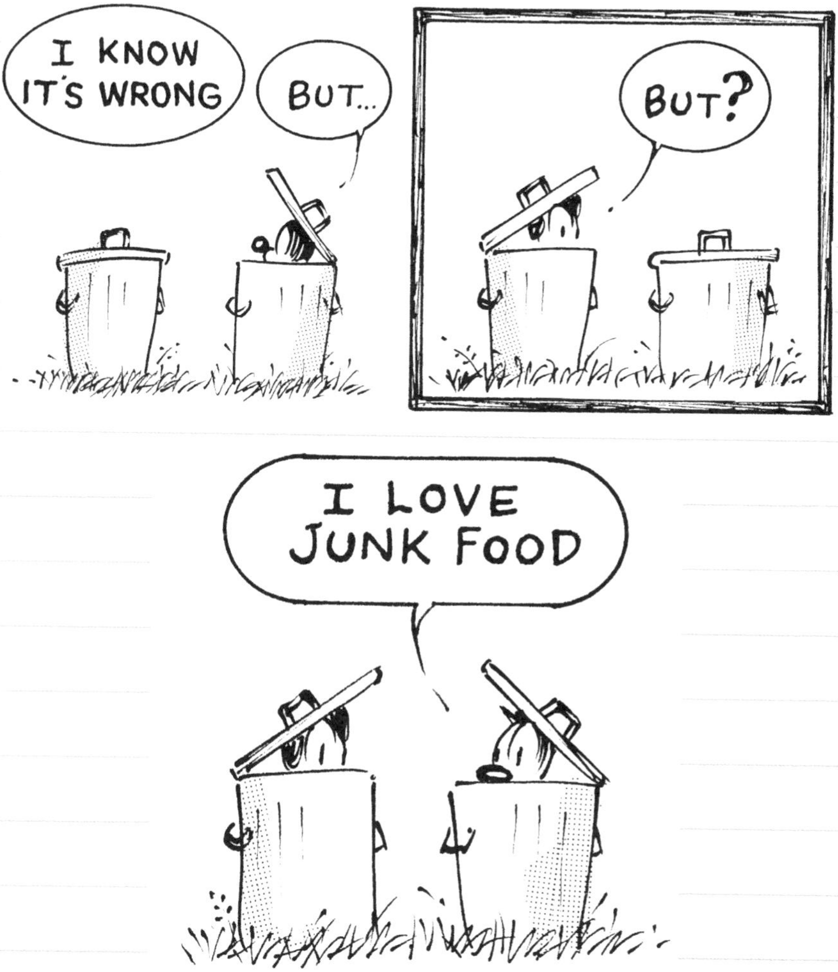
I KNOW IT'S WRONG
BUT...
BUT?
I LOVE JUNK FOOD

WHAT'CHA DOING, MOOCH?
I'M TRYING MY HAND AT PHOTOSHYNTHESIS
HOW'S IT GOING?
YOU'RE BLOCKING MY LUNCH.

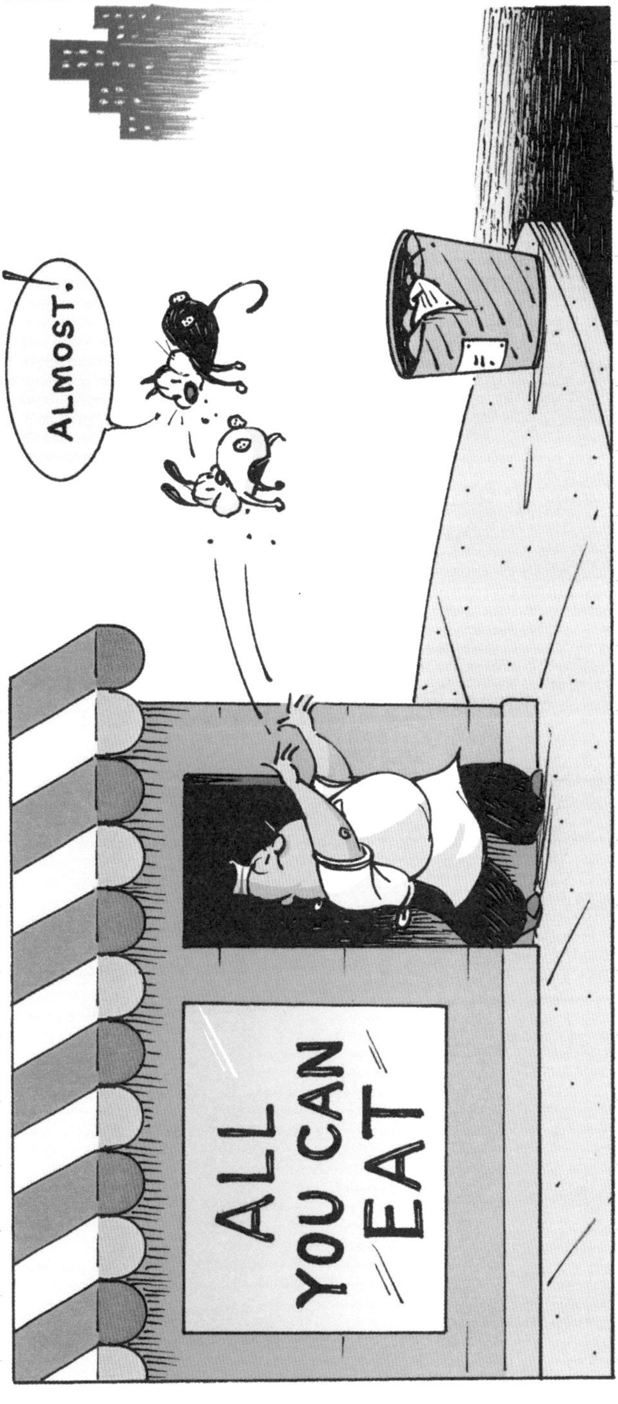
ALL YOU CAN EAT
ALMOST!

I HAVE TO GO SHTART DINNER.

MEOW
MEOW
MEOW
MEOW

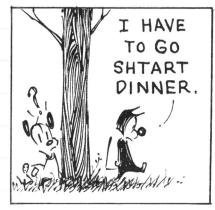

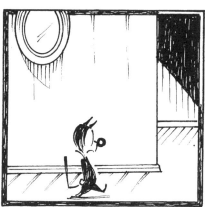

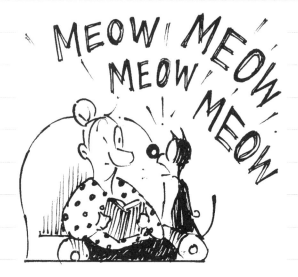

EARL-
WHAT'S MY TAIL DOING?
KIND OF SWISHING AROUND, MOOCH.
I THOUGHT SHO.
HE'S ALWAYS DOING SHTUFF BEHIND MY BACK.

ZIP
ZAP
I DON'T KNOW WHY I DO THIS EITHER.

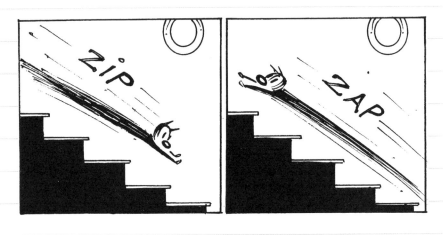

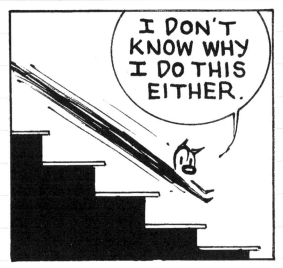

I CAN'T FIND MY DYED EGG WITH THE PAINTED FACE!
THAT SHOULD BE A NICE SHURPRIZE.

WHY?
WHY?
WHY?
WHY?
WHY?
WHY?
WHY?
WHY?
WHY?
WHY!?!
WHY DID `WE´ CHANGE KITTY LITTER BRANDS!?!

MOOCH!
ARE YOU ENJOYING MY DINNER?
NOT PARTICULARLY.

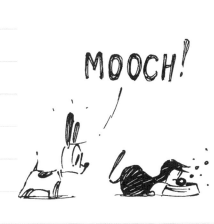

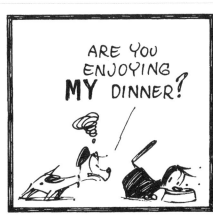

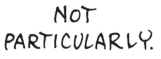

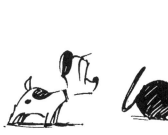

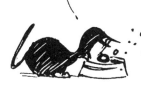

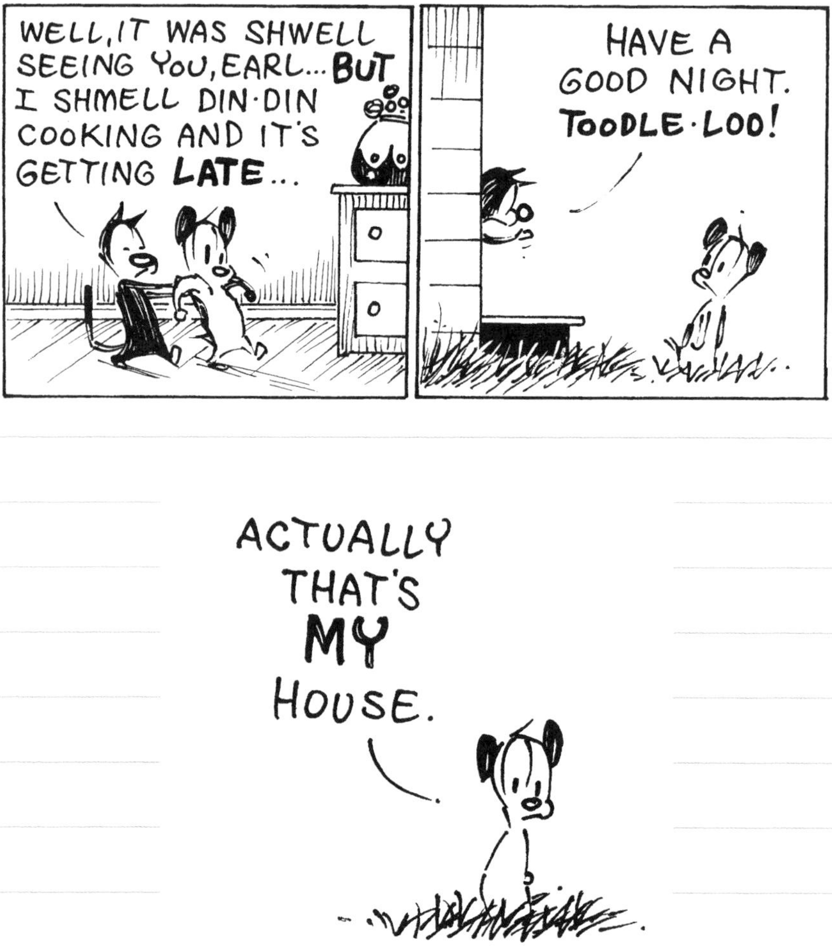
WELL, IT WAS SHWELL SEEING YOU, EARL... BUT I SHMELL DIN-DIN COOKING AND IT'S GETTING LATE...
HAVE A GOOD NIGHT. TOODLE-LOO!
ACTUALLY THAT'S MY HOUSE.

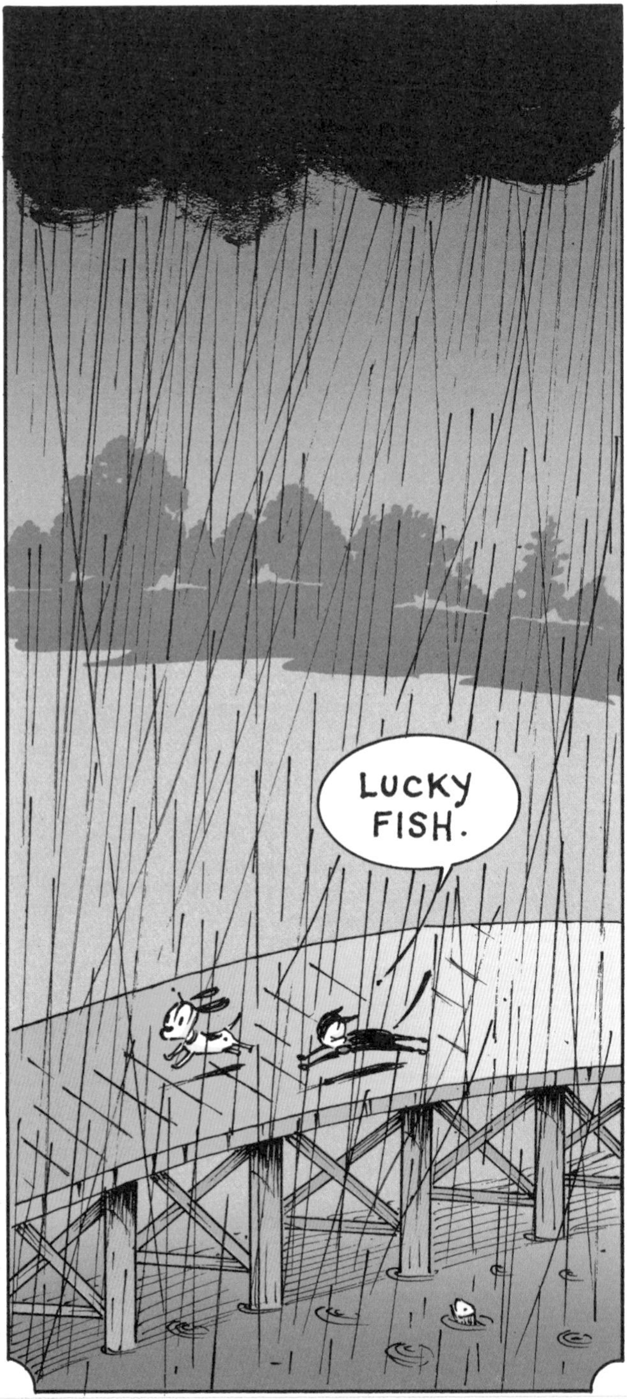
LUCKY FISH.

LITTLE PINK SOCK
LITTLE PINK
SOCK
?
HEY–THIS
IS A PRIVATE
CONCERT.

ooooo
SMOOCH
SHMIK SHMAK
KISSH
THE PRICE OF BEAUTY.

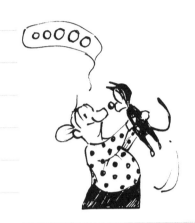

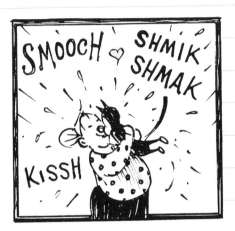

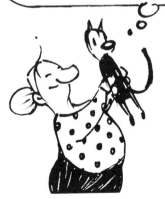

AAIEE! MOOCHIE!
WHAT ARE YOU DOING!?!
I THOUGHT I WAS HAVING FUN.

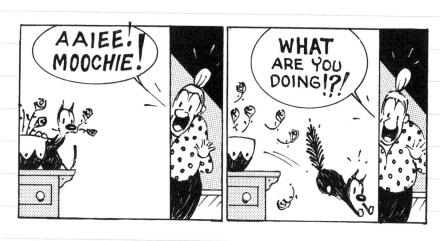

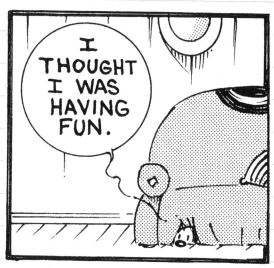

LOOK, MOOCH— TODAY THERE'S NOT A CLOUD IN THE SKY.
WOW
WHERE ARE THEY?

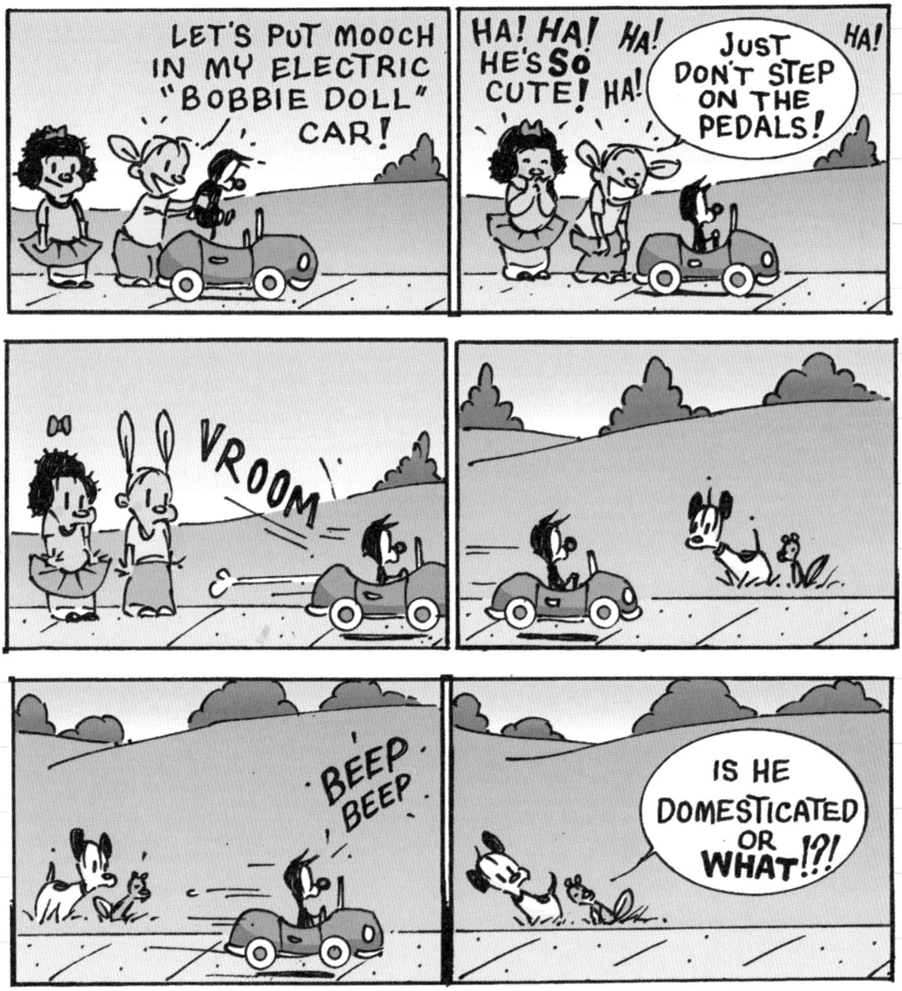
LET'S PUT MOOCH IN MY ELECTRIC "BOBBIE DOLL" CAR!
HA! HA! HA! HE'S SO CUTE! HA! HA!
JUST DON'T STEP ON THE PEDALS!
VROOM
BEEP BEEP
IS HE DOMESTICATED OR WHAT!?!

GANGWAY, EARL! I'M SHTUCK IN A RUN-AWAY ELECTRIC 'BOBBIE DOLL' CAR!!!
HELP.
I CAN'T FIND THE RADIO!

HOP IN, EARL! DOOZY'S ELECTRIC KIDDIE CAR IS OUT OF CONTROL!
I SHOULD BE DRIVING, MOOCH!
WHY?!
I HAVE A LICENSE

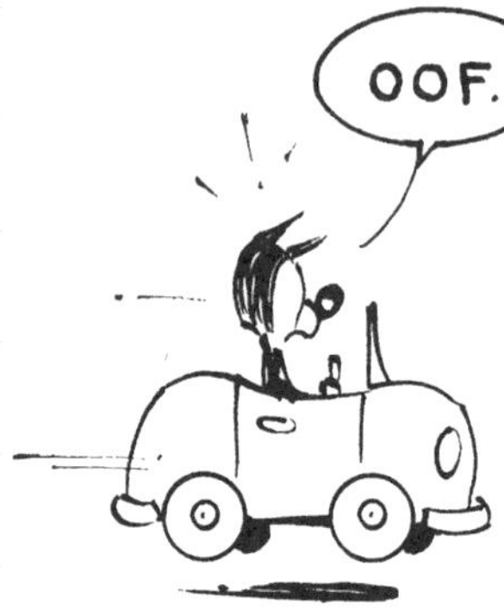
OOF.

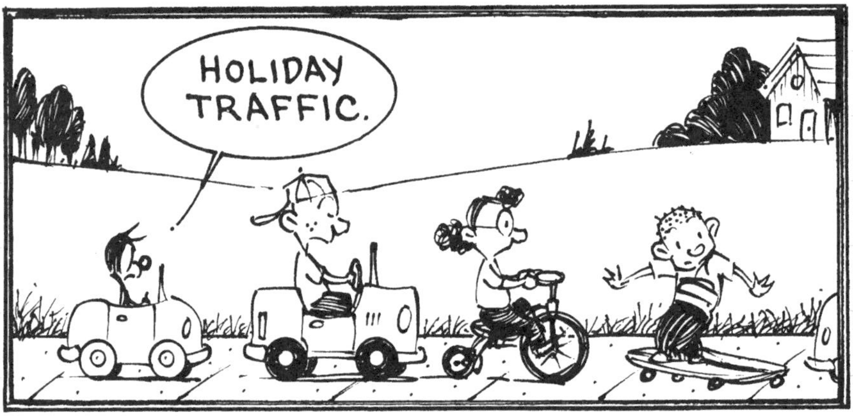
HOLIDAY TRAFFIC.

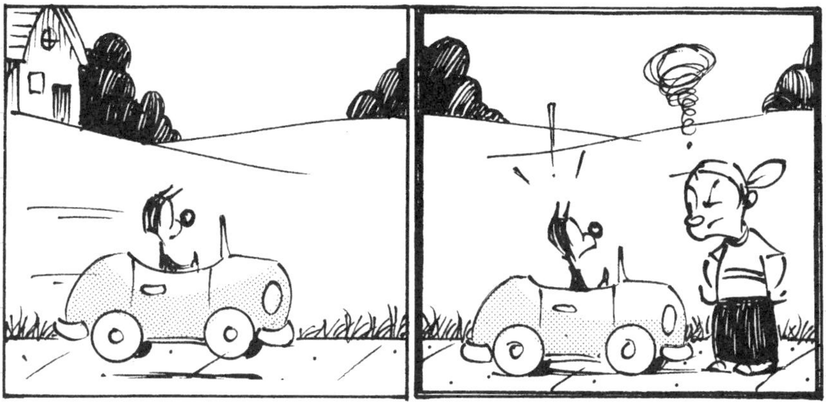

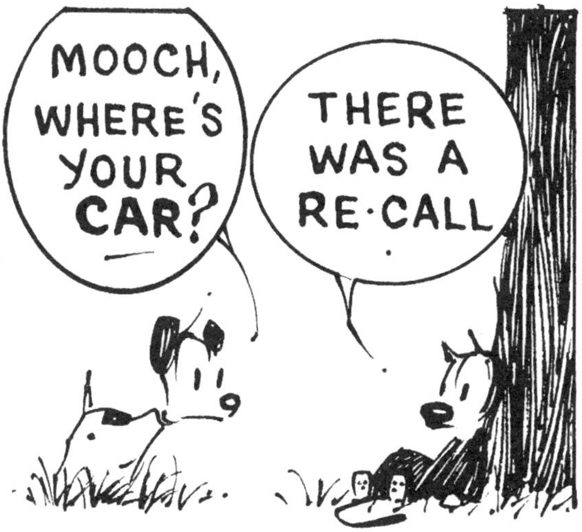
MOOCH, WHERE'S YOUR CAR?
THERE WAS A RE·CALL

♫ LITTLE ♫ PINK SOCK LIT...
♫ ...TLE ♫ PINK SOCK

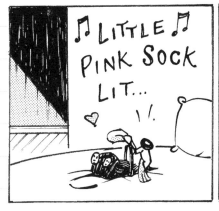

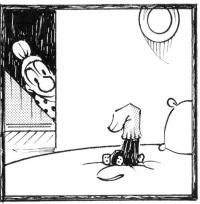

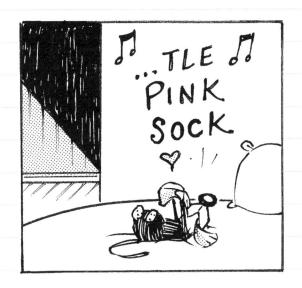

FOO.
WHY IS IT SO HOT?
WE'RE TILTING A LITTLE CLOSER TO THE SUN.
OH.

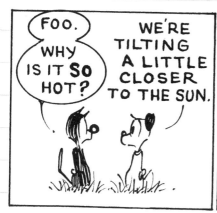

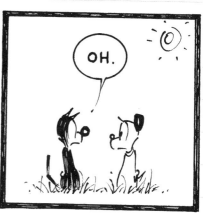

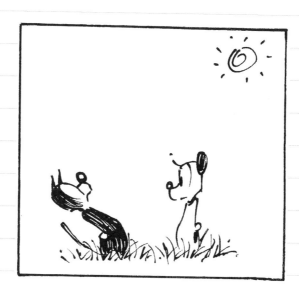

HEY, MOOCH- WE'RE **ALL** GOING DOWN THE SHORE!
Z·Z·Z
FINALLY!
I COULD USE A VACATION.

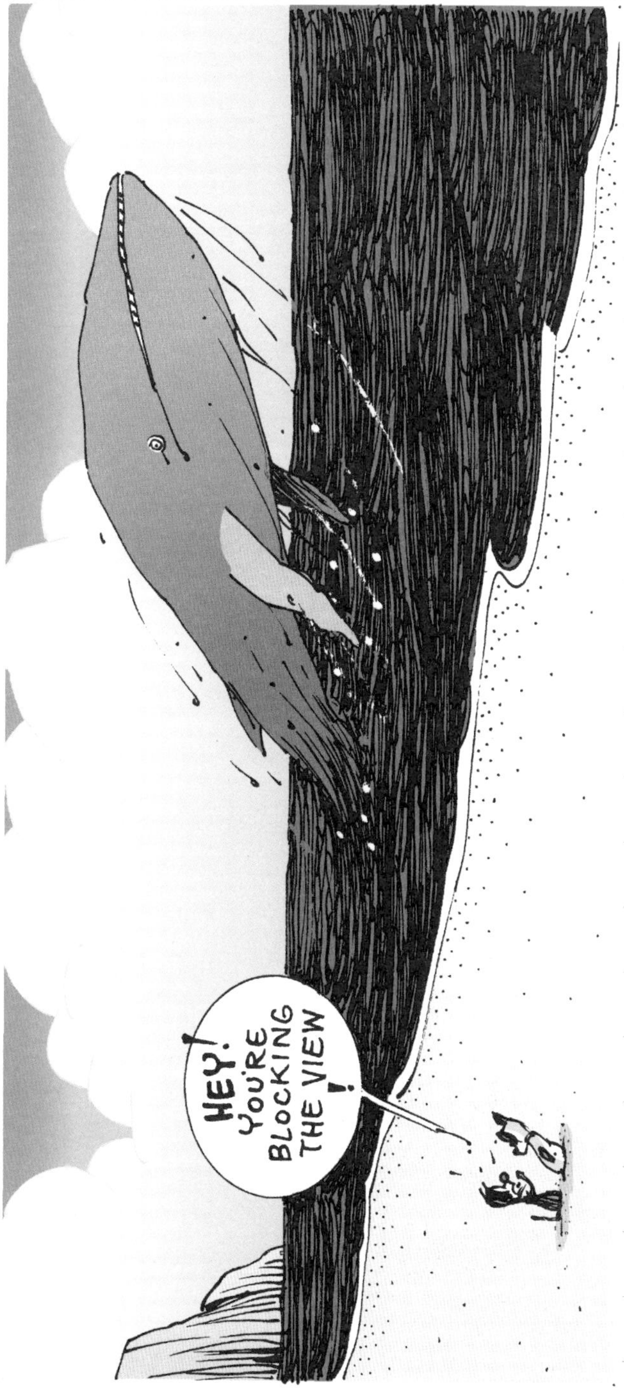
HEY! YOU'RE BLOCKING THE VIEW!

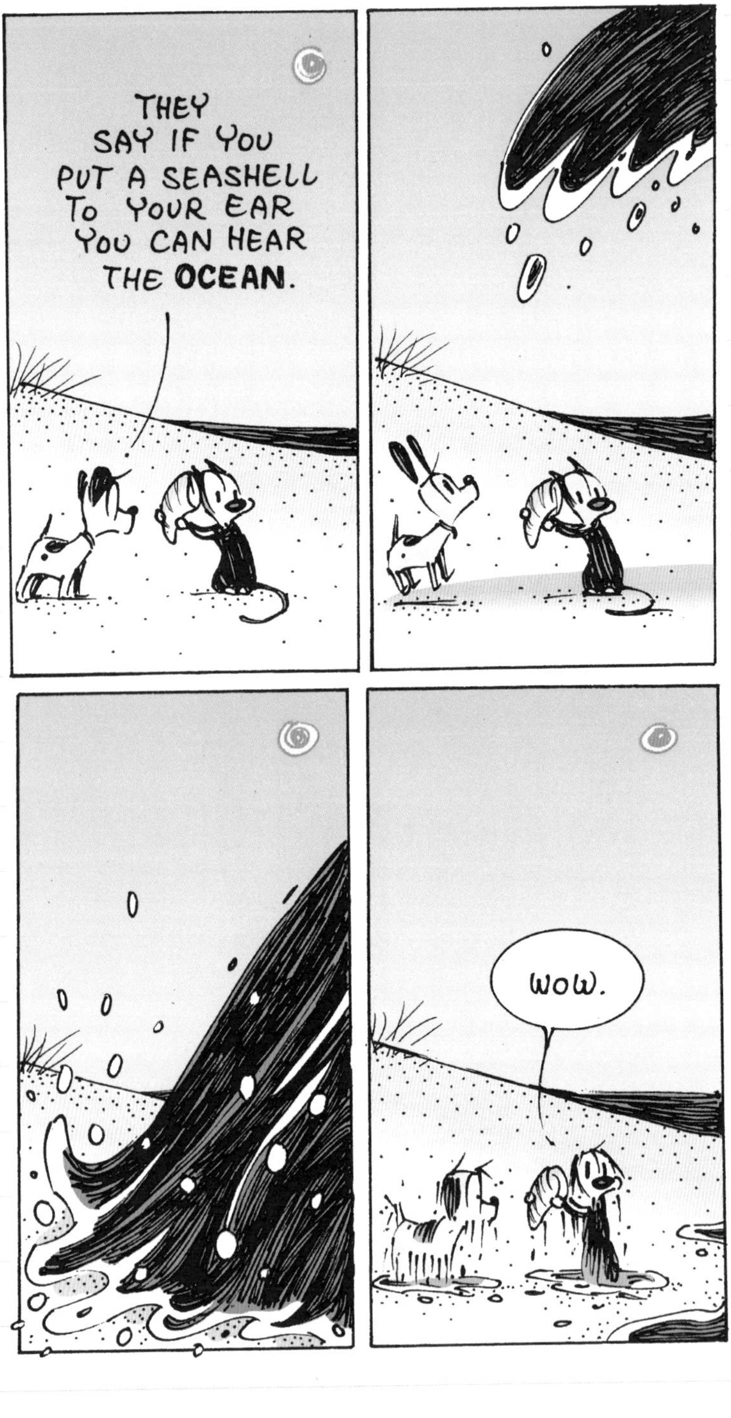
THEY SAY IF YOU PUT A SEASHELL TO YOUR EAR YOU CAN HEAR THE **OCEAN**.
WOW.

HEY, BIP, BOP–DID YOU MISS US?
BONK
BONK
NOT IF I CAN HELP IT.

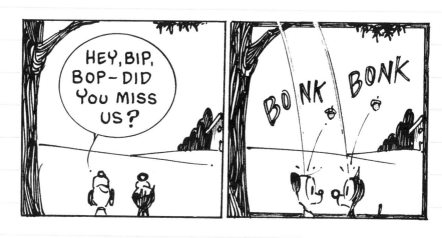

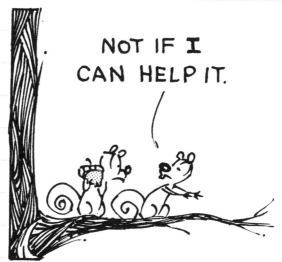

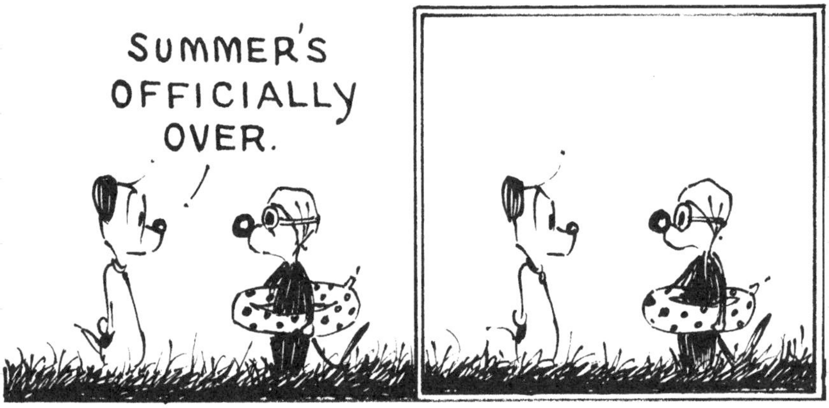
SUMMER'S OFFICIALLY OVER.

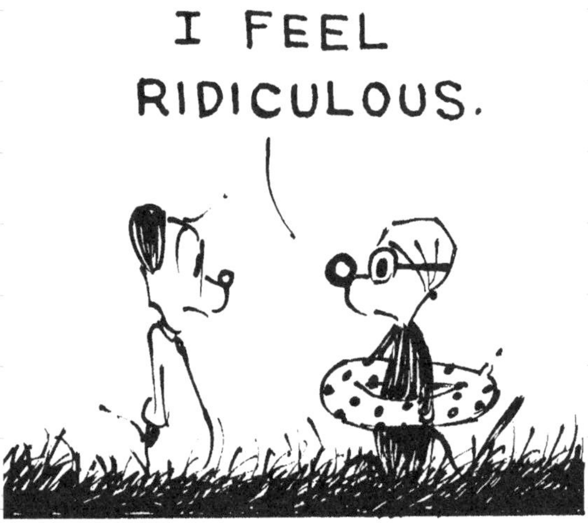
I FEEL RIDICULOUS.

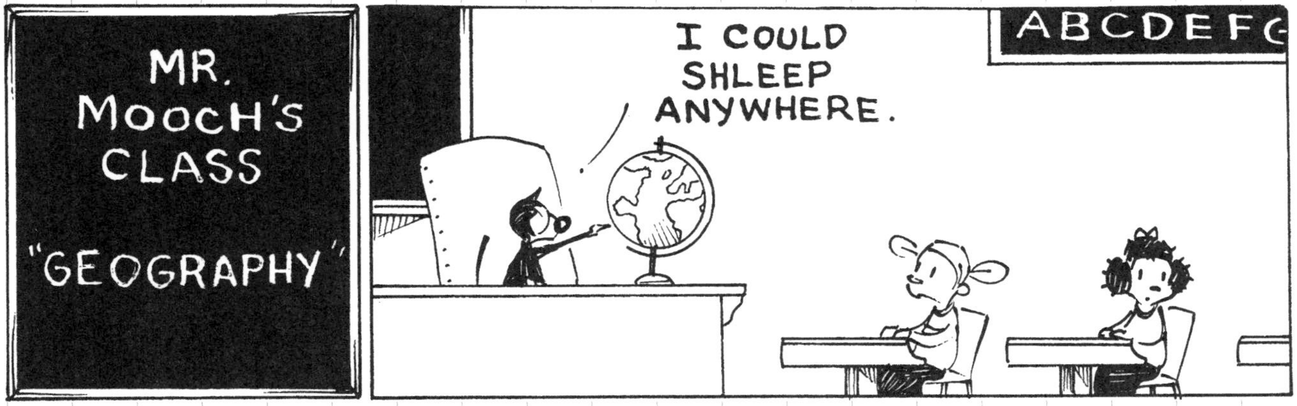
MR. MOOCH'S CLASS
"GEOGRAPHY"
I COULD SHLEEP ANYWHERE.
ABCDEFG

♫ LITTLE PINK ♫ SOCK LITTLE PINK SOCK
LIFE IS GOOD.

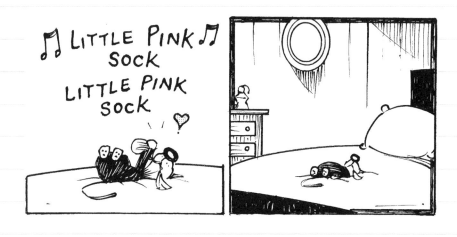

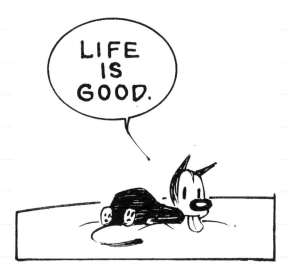

THE LEAVES WILL BE CHANGING COLOR SOON.
YESH.
I TRIED THAT ONCE.
IT'S **NOT** AS EASY AS IT LOOKS.

LOOK OUT! THE WHOLE THING SHMIGHT BLOW!

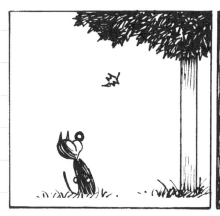

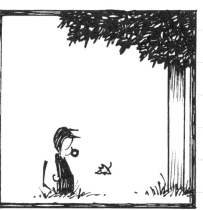

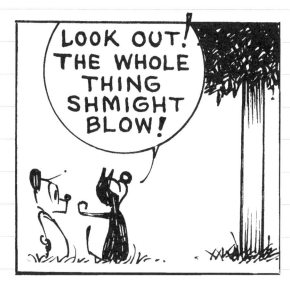

LOOK, MOOCH — A **NEW** BED!
!
GREAT...
LET ME KNOW HOW YOU LIKE IT.

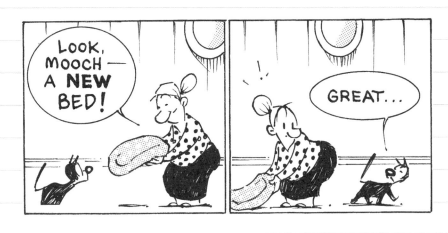

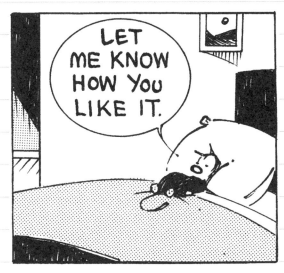

HEY! LET'S HAVE A SHTARE CONTEST! FIRST ONE TO BLINK IS **OUT**.
GOOD LUCK.

SHTARE CONTEST! FIRST ONE TO BLINK IS **OUT**!
MADE YOU LOOK.

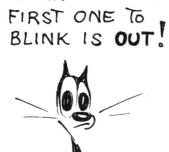

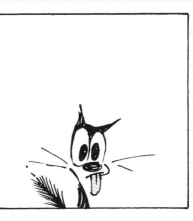

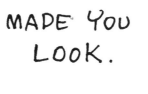

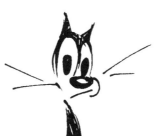

NO ONE BEATS ME AT A SHTARING CONTEST!
NO, I DIDN'T!!!

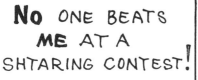

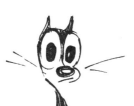

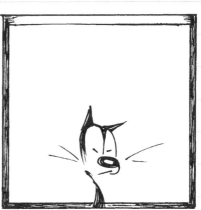

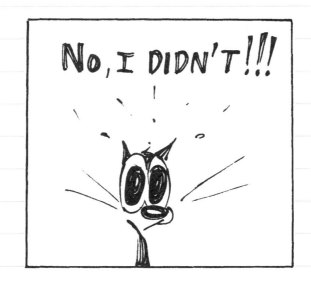

IT'S L.P.S. TIME!
LITTLE PINK SOCK
LITTLE PINK SOCK
WE'RE B.F.F.

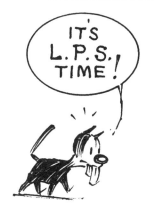

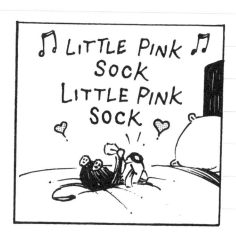

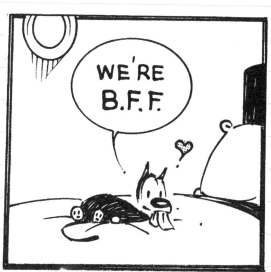

BONK
YOU, PAL, HAVE A MAJOR PROBLEM!
HE'S RIGHT.
I'M OUT OF NUTS.

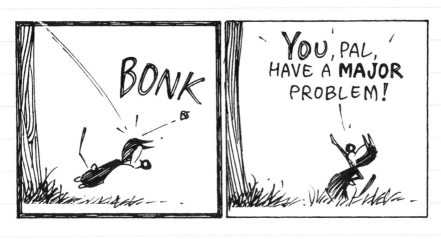

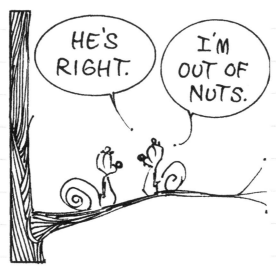

IT SHMAY SHEEM LIKE MY WATER DISH, BUT IT'S MY NEW SHQUIRREL DEFENSE!
LOOK! IT'S ABSHOLUTELY FOOL PROOF!
BONK

THOSE SHQUIRRELS ARE NUTS! THEY LEAVE ME NO CHOICE BUT TO SHTAY IN TODAY. WHAT ELSHE CAN I DO !?!
BONK
CLOSE THE WINDOWS.

THAT KID'S BEEN WAITING AT **YOUR** FRONT DOOR **ALL** DAY.

HA!
LOOK AT YOU...
ALL SHOFT AND MUSHY!
WHO'S LAUGHING NOW?

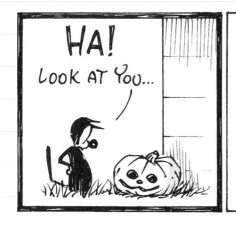

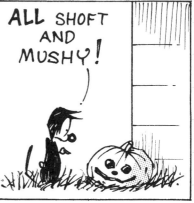

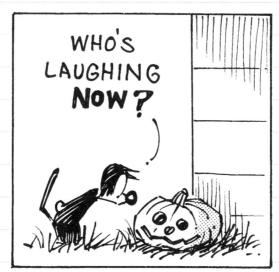

ACK!!! SHMILLIE KNITTED ME AN ICKY HAT!!!
FOO! I SAW HER KNITTING ALL WEEK—I KNEW THIS WAS COMING!!!
YUP...
NOBODY CAN PULL THE WOOL OVER YOUR EYES.

AAAIIEE
AAAAIIEE
AAAAIIEE
I TOLD YOU IT WAS COLD OUT.
BRRR.

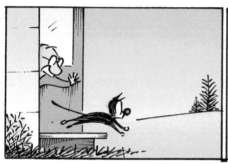

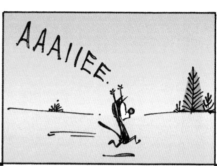

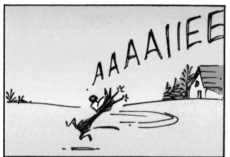

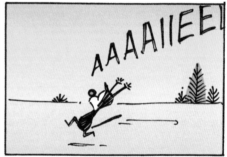

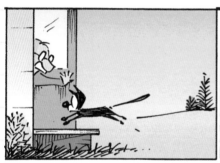

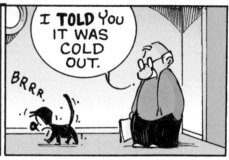

LOOK AT THAT!
IT'S SNOWING!

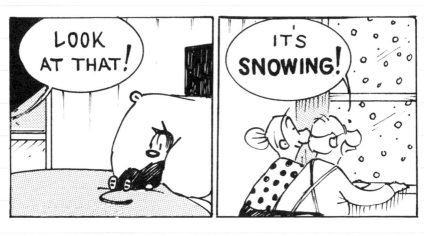

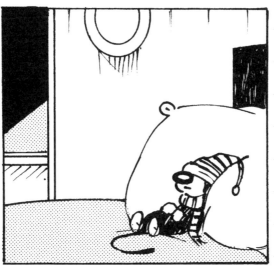

I'M ALLERGIC TO SNOW.

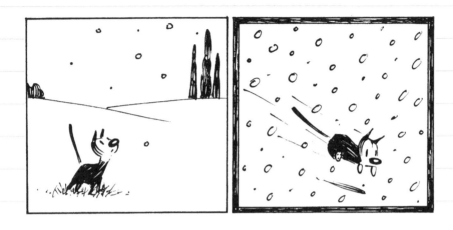

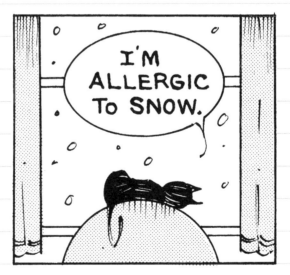

LITTLE PINK SOCK LITTLE PINK SOCK
PIFF
POOF
PHOOP
SOCK SOLO.

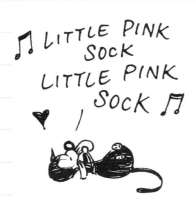

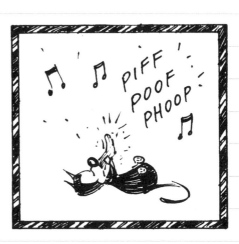

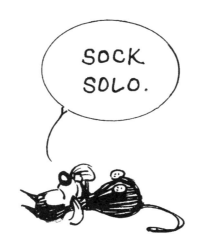

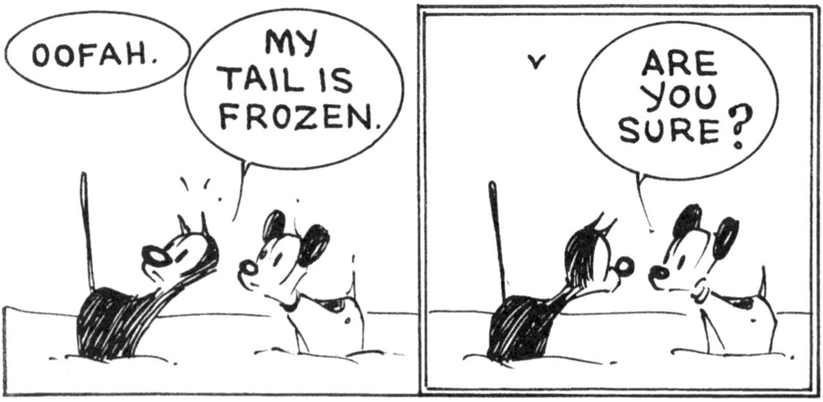
OOFAH.
MY TAIL IS FROZEN.
ARE YOU SURE?

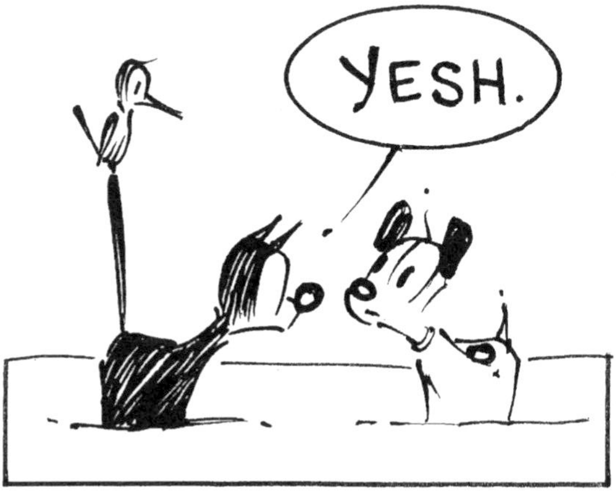
YESH.

BRRRR...
I FORGOT MY MITTEN!
YOU MEAN MITTENS!
WHAT DID YOU SAY?

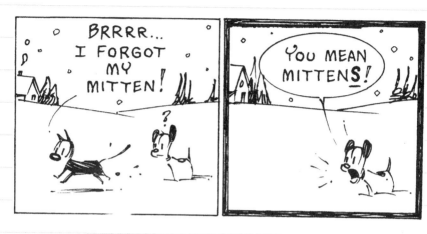

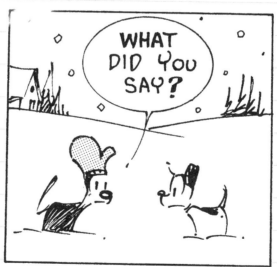

MUTTS
LET'S DO IT AGAIN.
YESH.

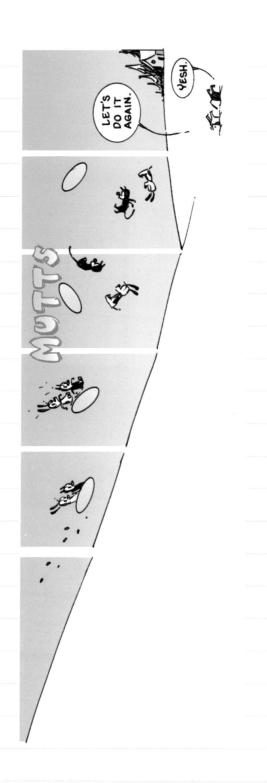

SO, EARL, WE'RE GOING TO TRY TO HIBERNATE ALL THE WAY TO SHPRING
YUP.
OOF.
THAT COULD BE TOUGH.
WHY?
I SHMIGHT RUN OUT OF DREAMS.

HEY! ARE YOU SNORING !?!
NOT ME.

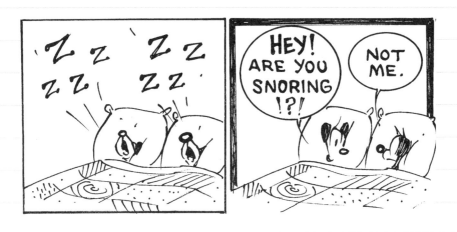

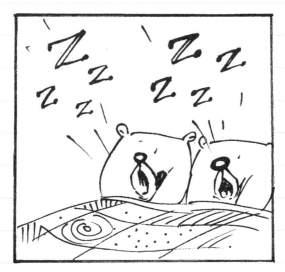

Earl's Diary

Dear Diary
TODAY IS
LOVELY.

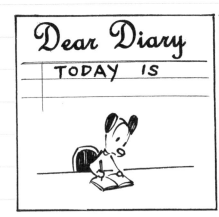

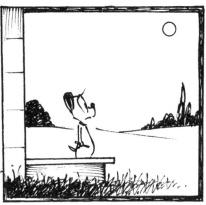

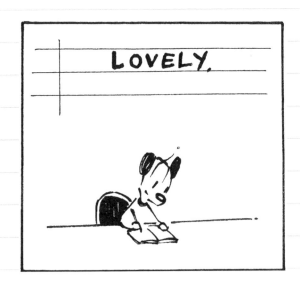

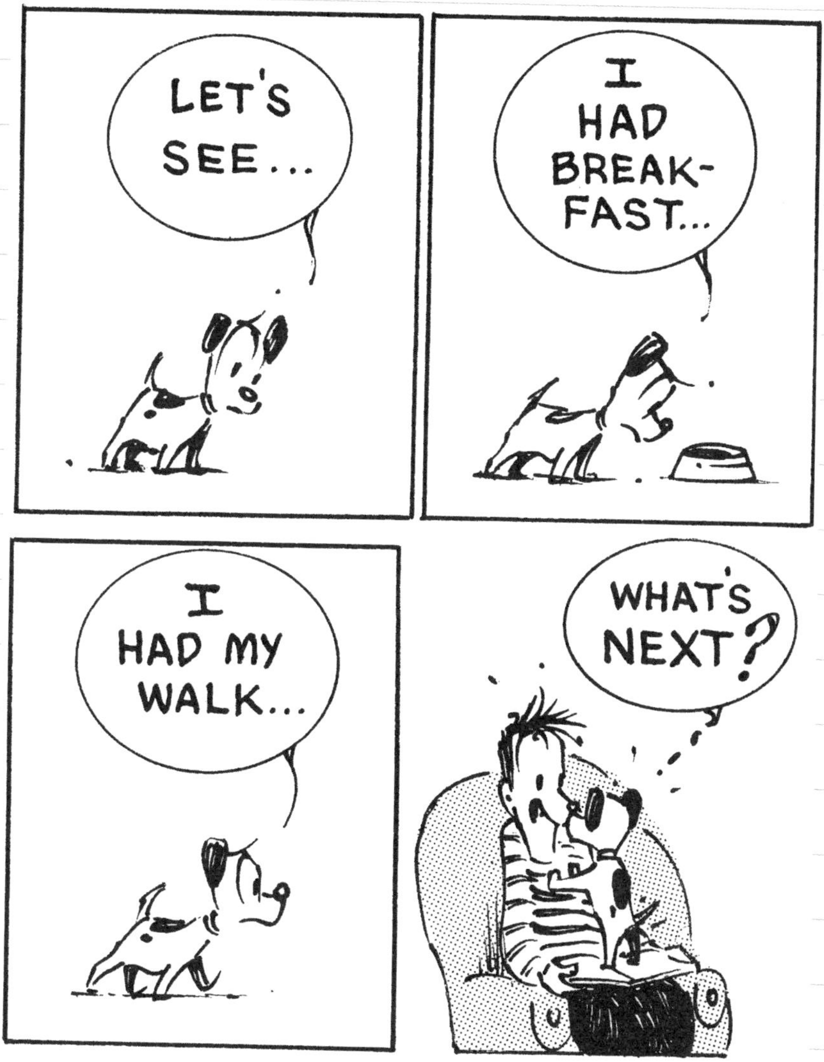
LET'S SEE...
I HAD BREAK-FAST...
I HAD MY WALK...
WHAT'S NEXT?

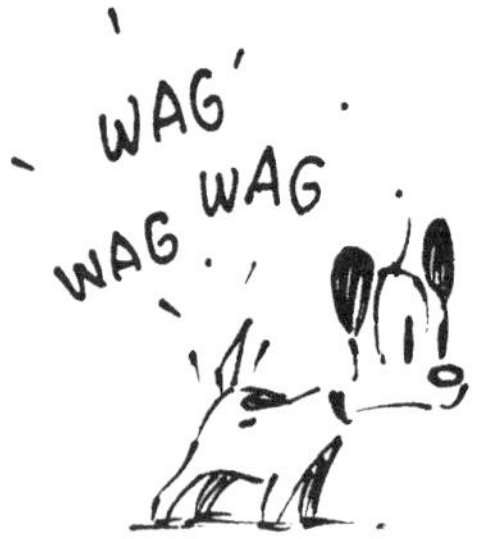
WAG
WAG WAG

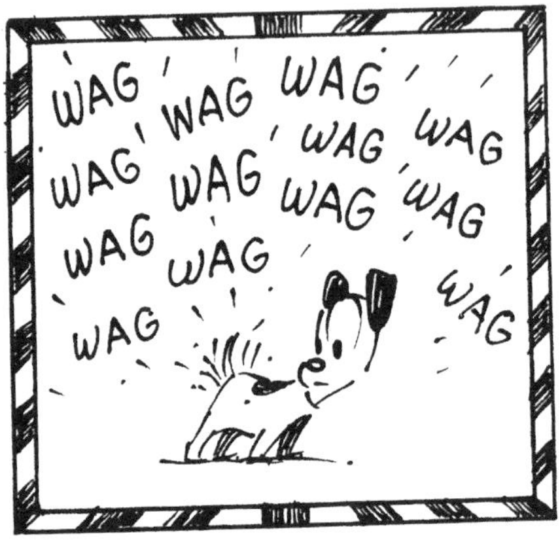
WAG WAG WAG
WAG WAG WAG
WAG WAG WAG WAG
WAG WAG
WAG WAG

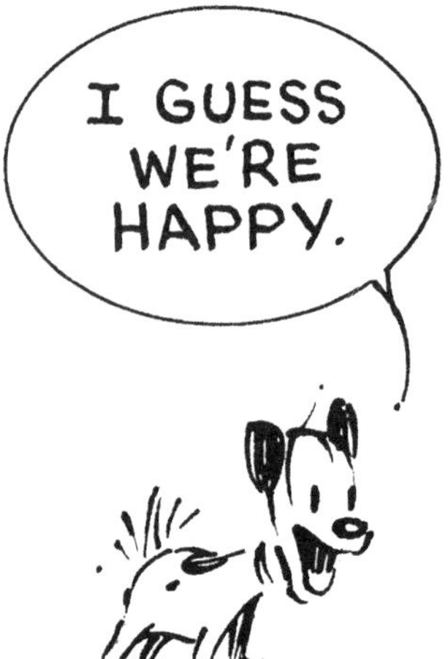
I GUESS WE'RE HAPPY.

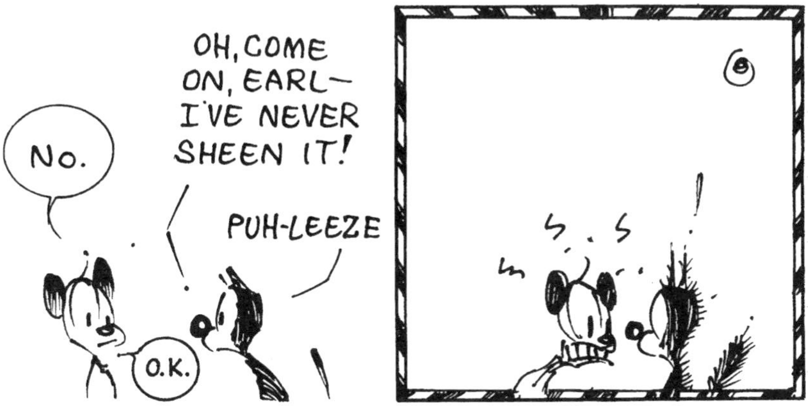
No.
OH, COME ON, EARL— I'VE NEVER SHEEN IT!
O.K.
PUH-LEEZE

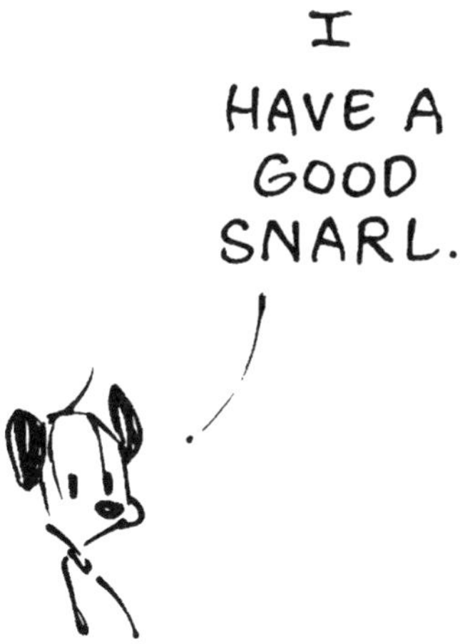
I HAVE A GOOD SNARL.

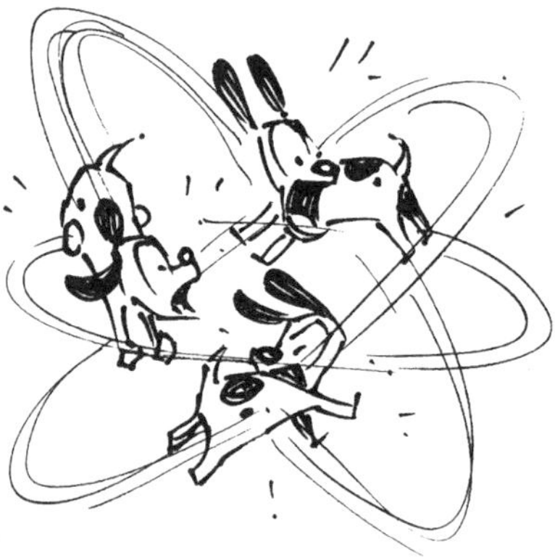

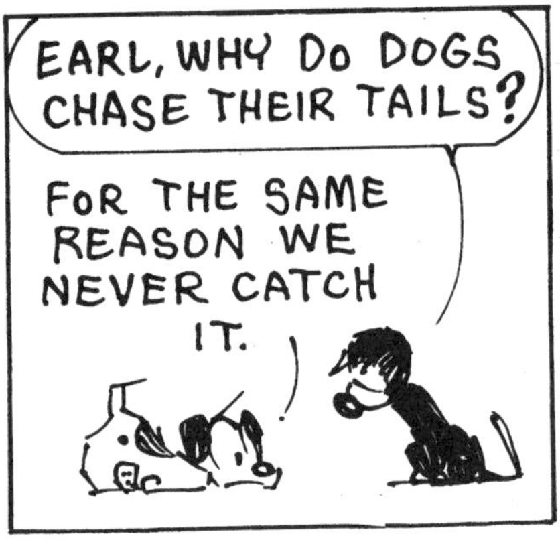
EARL, WHY DO DOGS CHASE THEIR TAILS?
FOR THE SAME REASON WE NEVER CATCH IT.

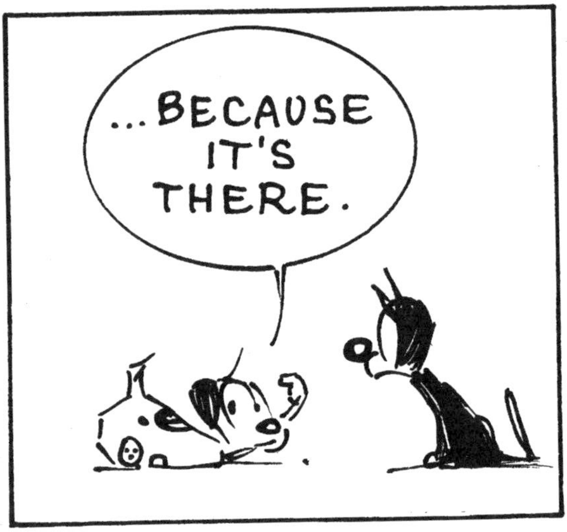
...BECAUSE IT'S THERE.

BARK BARK BARK BARK BARK
YOU'RE RIGHT, EARL.
THAT DOES FEEL GOOD.

SIGH...
THERE'S NEVER A BELLY RUB WHEN YOU NEED ONE.

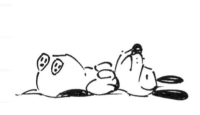

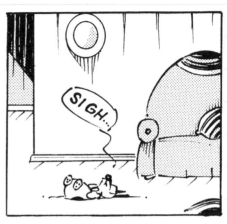

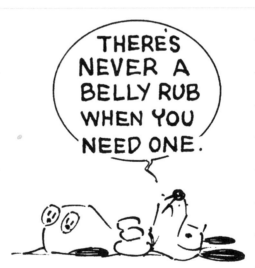

PAT
PAT
PAT
WELL?
IT DOES SHMAKE IT ALL BETTER

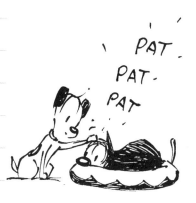

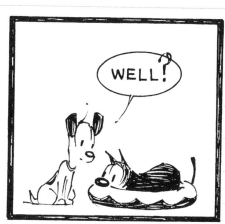

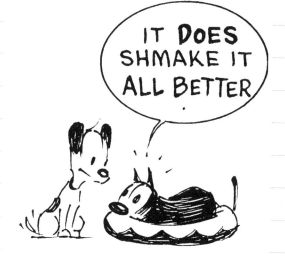

AUGH. I THINK I'M SICK.
HOW CAN YOU TELL?
MY NOSE ISN'T WET OR COLD.
I CAN FIX THAT.

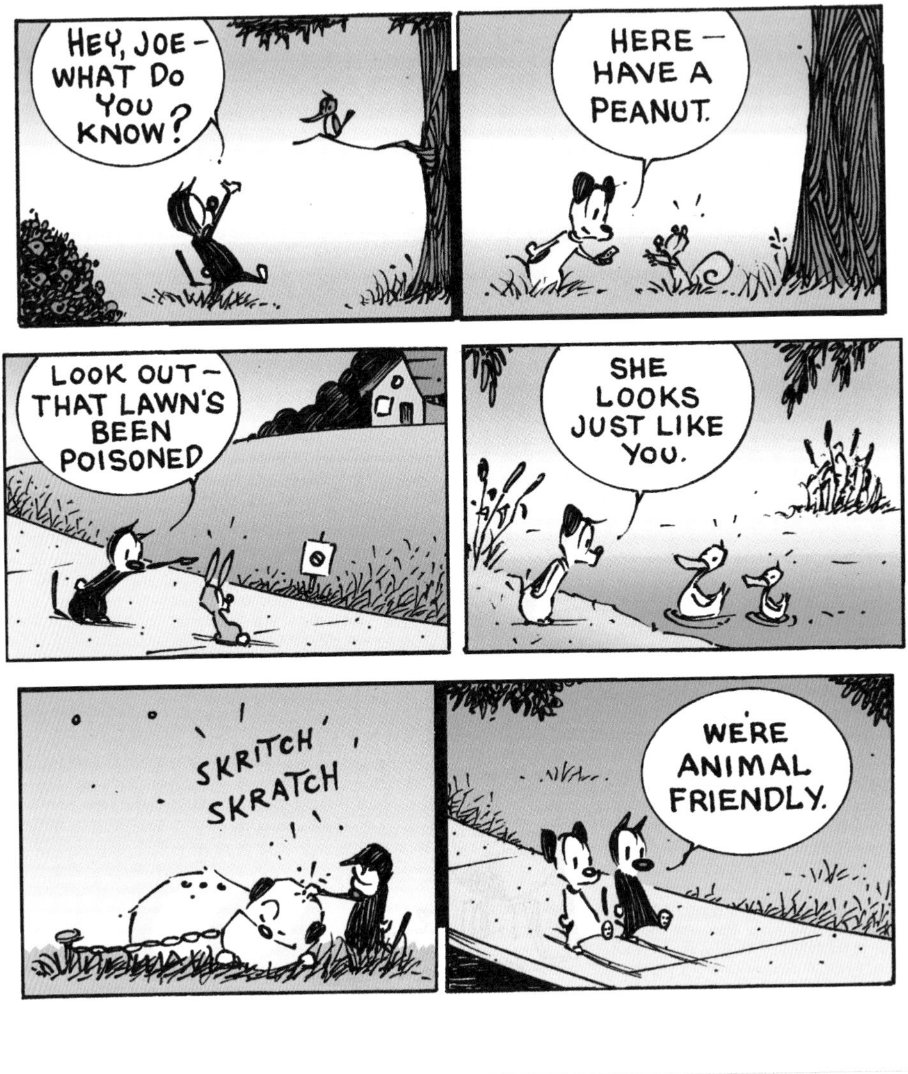
HEY, JOE - WHAT DO YOU KNOW?
HERE - HAVE A PEANUT.
LOOK OUT - THAT LAWN'S BEEN POISONED
SHE LOOKS JUST LIKE YOU.
SKRITCH SKRATCH
WE'RE ANIMAL FRIENDLY.

GOING TO A RESTAURANT WAS A GREAT IDEA, MOOCH!
YESH! NOW IF ONLY WE CAN GET SHOME SHERVICE.
AAAAIEEEE
I THINK I CAUGHT OUR WAITRESS'S EYE.

THIS IS MY "SO HAPPY TO SEE YOU AGAIN" FACE
AGAIN!

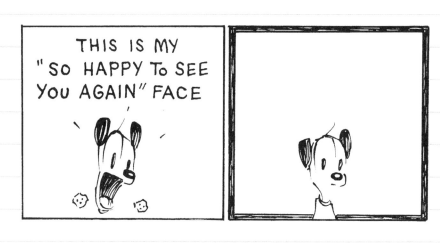

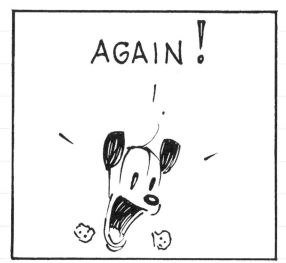

OZZIE!
Lick
Lick Lick
Lick Lick
Lick Lick
Lick
HEY!
WHO HAD PIZZA WITHOUT ME!?!

WHO WANTS TO GO FOR A WALK?
ME!
?
WHO ELSE!?!

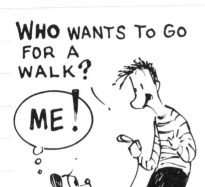

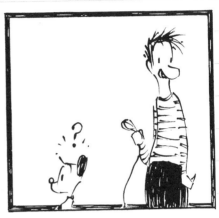

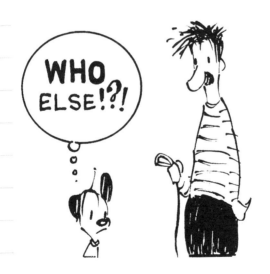

EVERY DOG SHOULD GO FOR A COMPLETE MEDICAL AT LEAST ONCE A YEAR.
DR. WOO
FOR GOOD HEALTH... FOR PEACE OF MIND...
FOR THE LOLLIPOP.

EARL, BABY!!!
WHAT A SHURPRIZE!
MOOCH—I JUST SAW YOU THIS MORNING!?!
HAS IT BEEN THAT LONG?

HEY, EARL—
HOW WAS
OBEDIENCE
SHCHOOL?
AWFUL.
NO ONE
DID A THING
I SAID.

RAIN, RAIN GO AWAY— COME AGAIN SOME OTHER DAY
NOW TRY IT WITH FEELING.

DO YOU WANT TO PLAY BALL?
DUH.

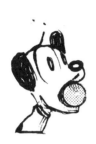

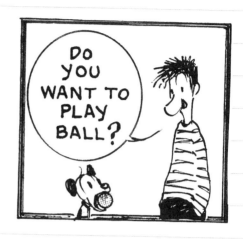

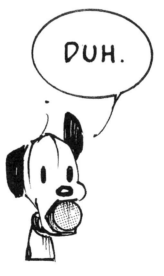

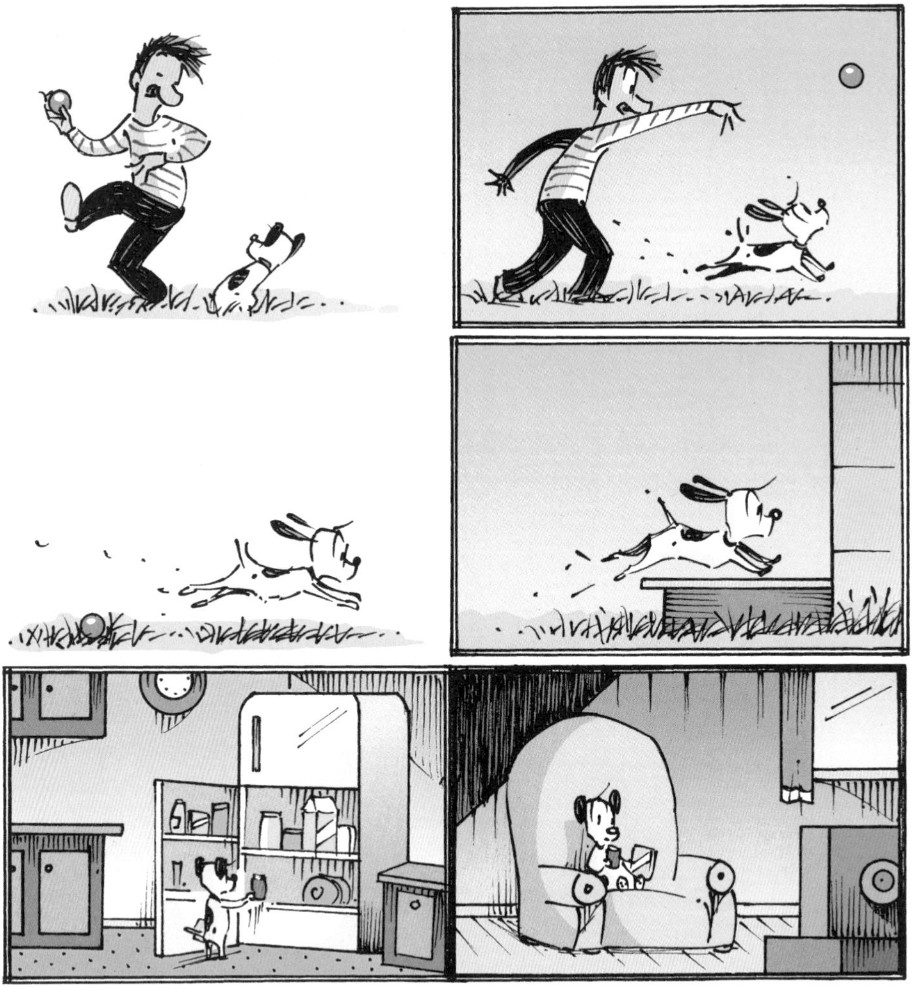

AHH... THE SWEET SONG OF SUMMER.
YESH! THE BIRDS SOUND DIVINE.
BIRDS?
I WAS TALKING ABOUT THE ICE CREAM TRUCK!

1. TAKE ONE DOG
AND ONE POOL
2. ADD WATER
3. AND STIR.

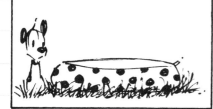

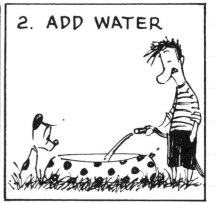

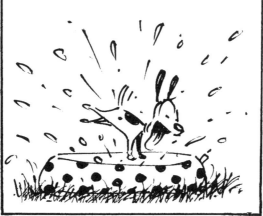

AHH...
PERFECT.
...EXCEPT FOR THAT WET DOG SMELL.

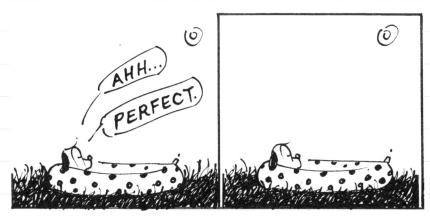

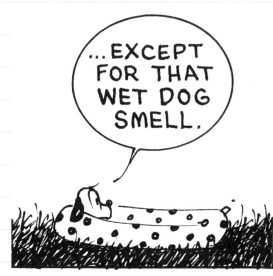

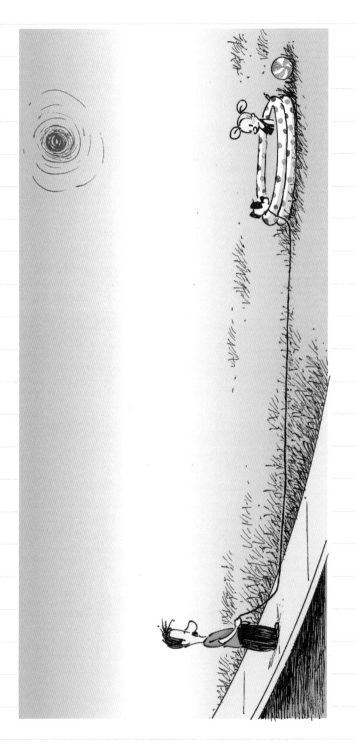

ARE WE LATE?

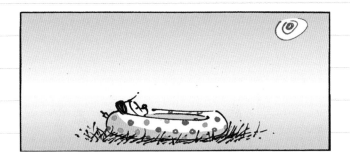

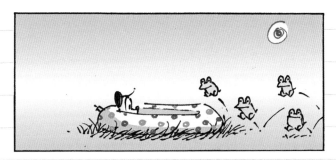

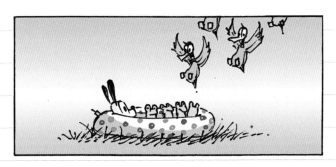

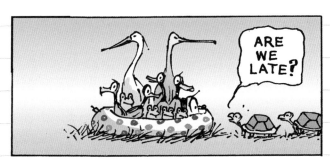

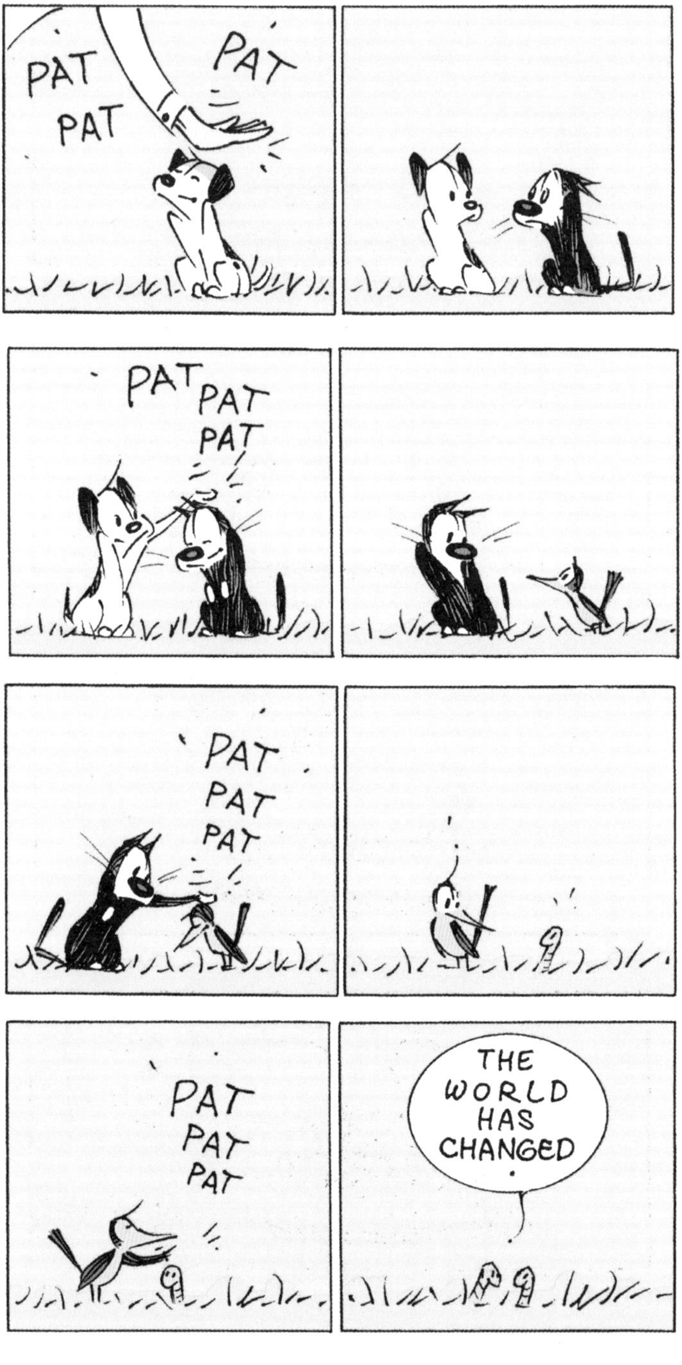
PAT
PAT
PAT
PAT
PAT
PAT
PAT
PAT
PAT
PAT
PAT
PAT
PAT
THE WORLD HAS CHANGED

THIS IS MY "ARE YOU GOING WITHOUT ME!?!" FACE
I DIDN'T THINK SO.

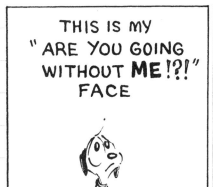

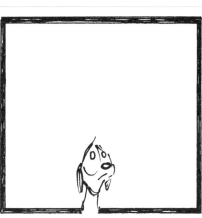

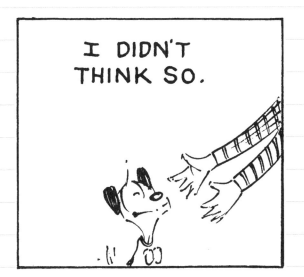

PAT
PAT
PAT
VACATIONS ARE GOOD.

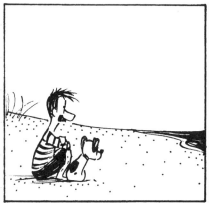

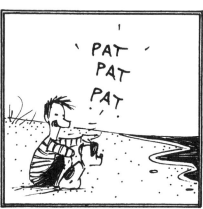

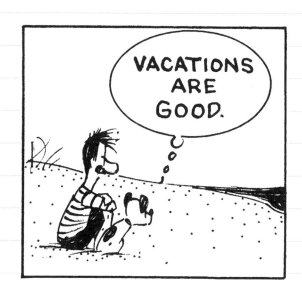

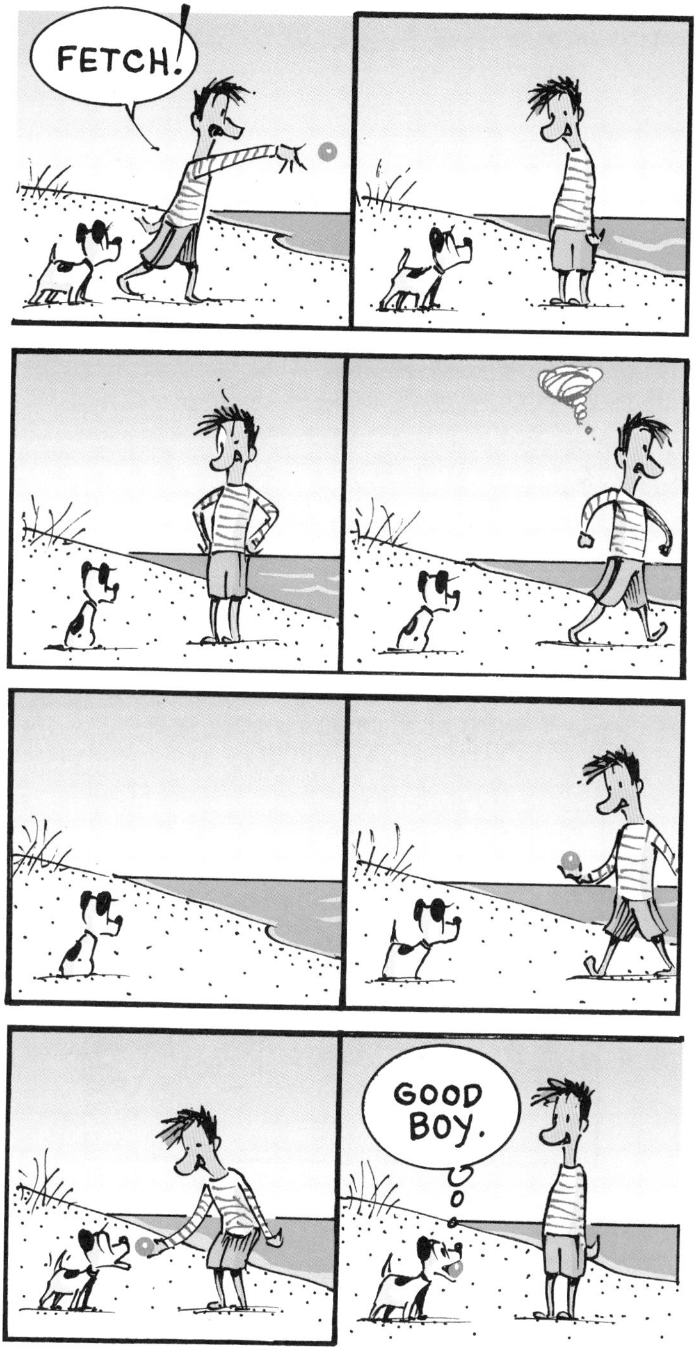
FETCH!
GOOD BOY.

AUGH! I HATE WHEN PEOPLE LITTER THE BEACH!
THOSE ARE SHELLS - MOOCH!
WHO'S BEEN EATING NUTS?

MIRRORS DON'T LIE.

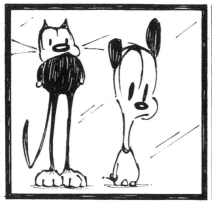

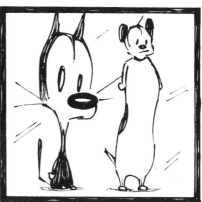

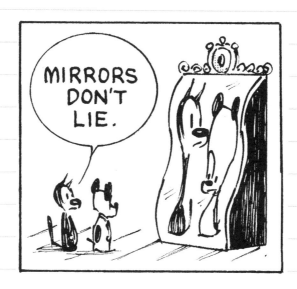

AUGH- IT'S TOO HOT, TOO HUMID, TOO BUGGY- AND THE SAND IS ITCHY-FOO!
WELL, MOOCH- THERE ARE ONLY TWO DAYS LEFT OF OUR VACATION.
REALLY?
GEE...
TIME REALLY FLIES WHEN YOU'RE HAVING FUN.

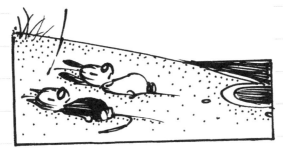

VACATION'S OVER! BACK TO SCHOOL!!!
HEY! NO DOGS OR CATS ALLOWED!

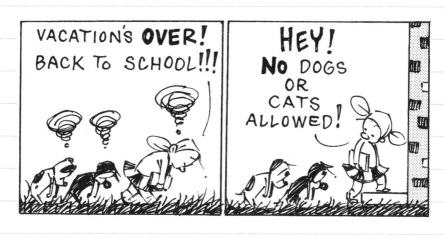

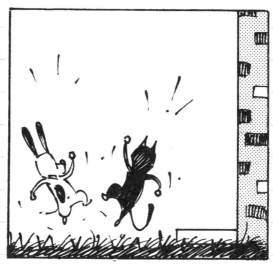

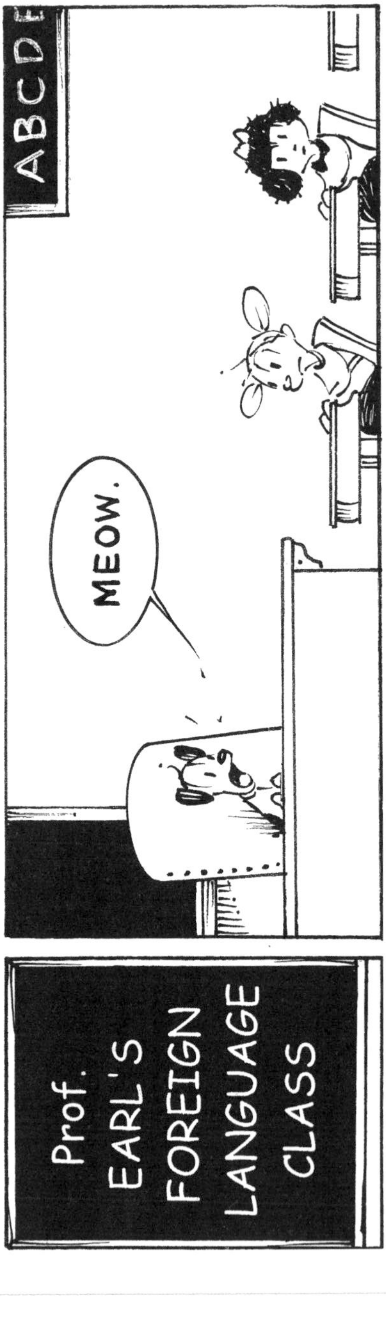
Prof.
EARL'S
FOREIGN
LANGUAGE
CLASS
ABCDE
MEOW.

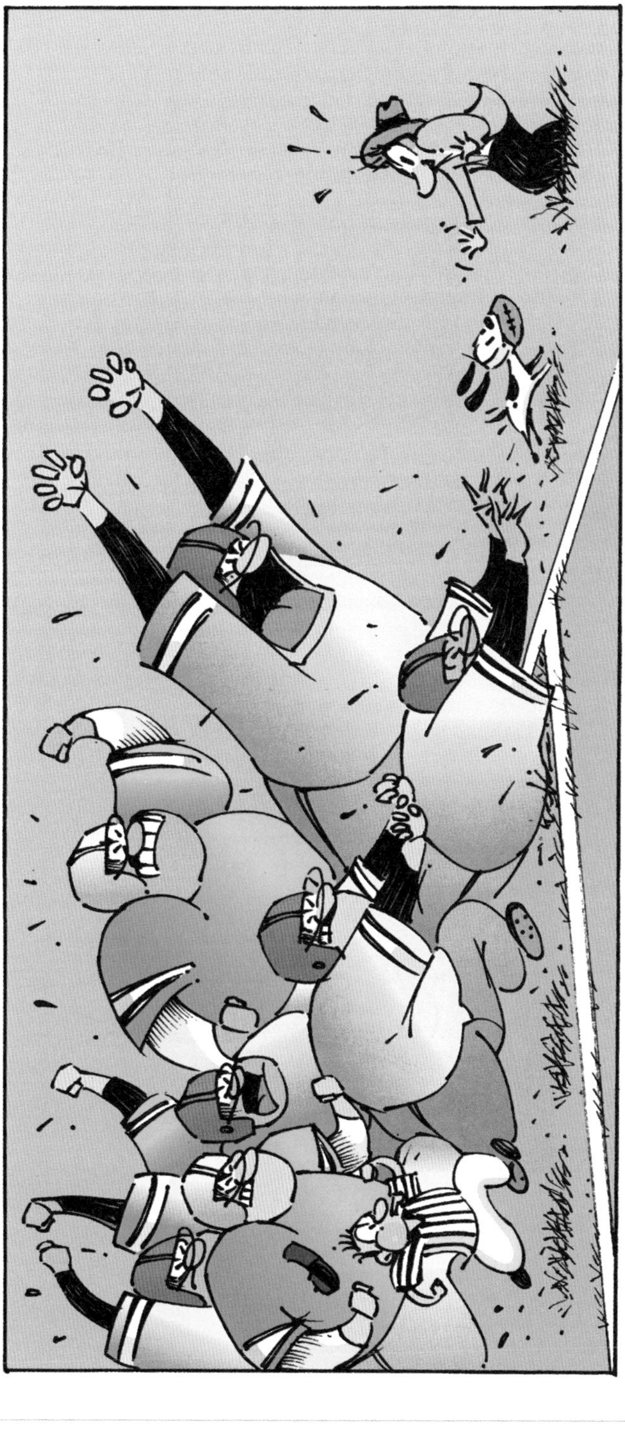

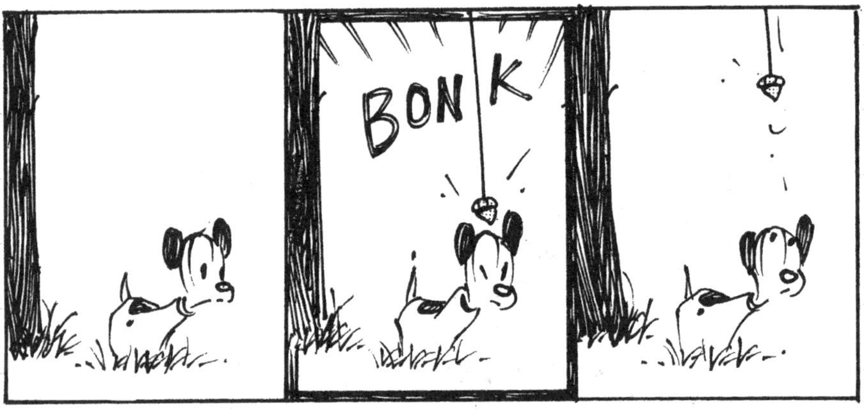
BONK

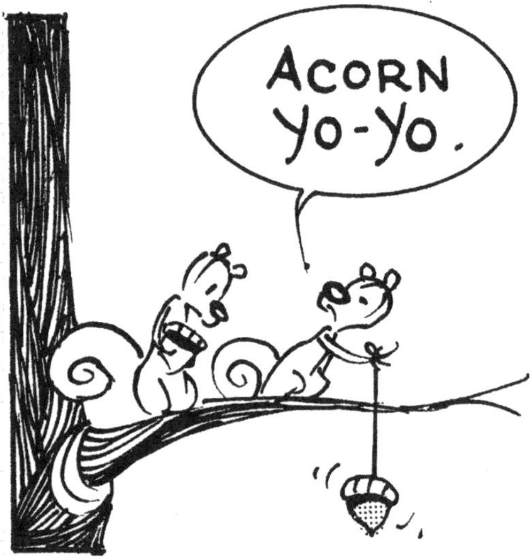
ACORN YO-YO.

WHATEVER
WHATEVER
HEY! YOU CAN'T WHATEVER MY WHATEVER!!!
WHATEVER
AUGH!
WHATEVER!
WHATEVER!!
WHATEVER!!!
WHATEVER.

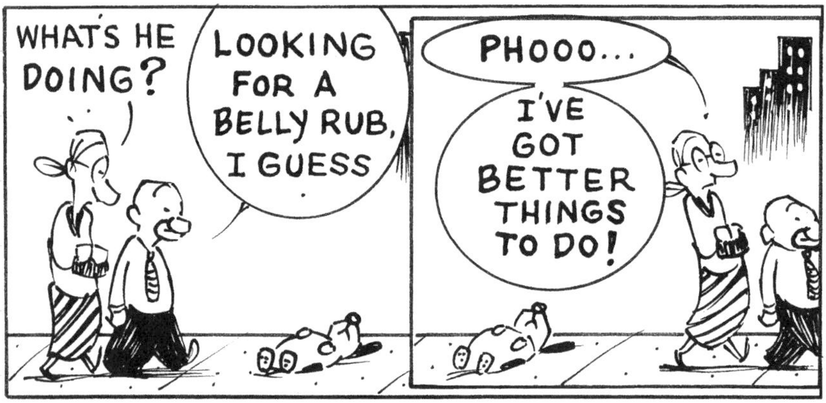
WHAT'S HE DOING?
LOOKING FOR A BELLY RUB, I GUESS
PHOOO...
I'VE GOT BETTER THINGS TO DO!

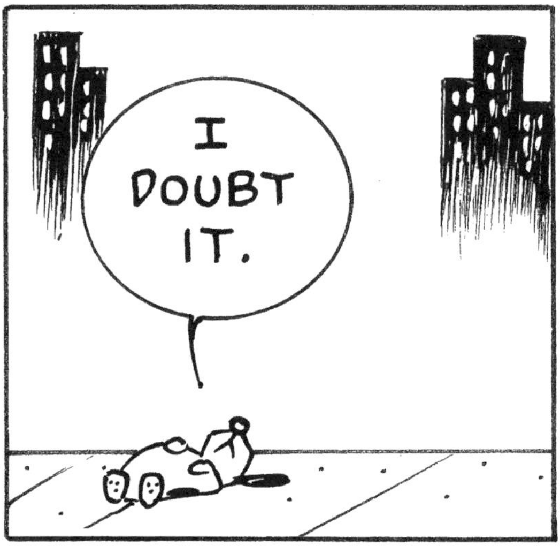
I DOUBT IT.

OOOH-YOU WITTLE CUTIE-GIVE ME A KISS!
SHMAK
I ALWAYS WANTED TO DO THAT.

GOOD DOG!
HA!
I COULD TELL HER SOME SHTORIES!

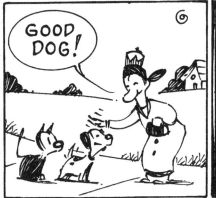

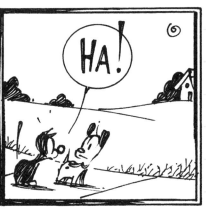

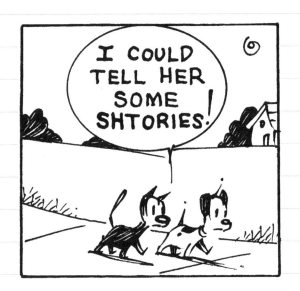

BE
KIND
TO
ANIMALS
WEEK
BELLY
RUB

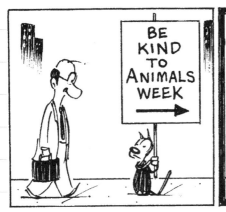

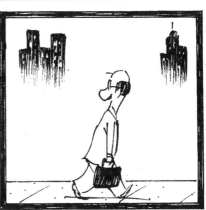

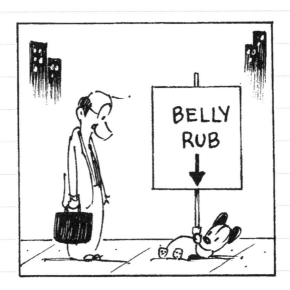

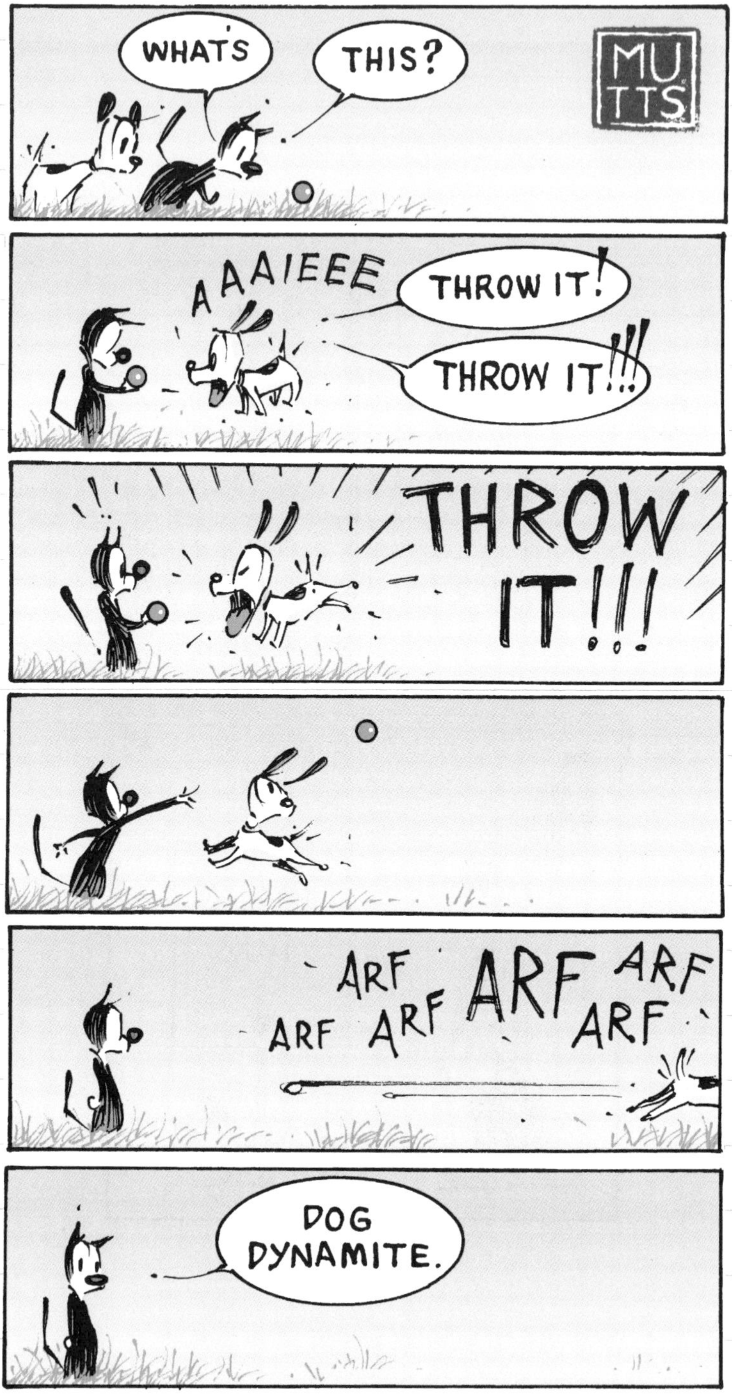
MUTTS
WHAT'S
THIS?
AAAIEEE
THROW IT!
THROW IT!!!
THROW IT!!!
ARF ARF ARF ARF ARF ARF
DOG DYNAMITE.

OOF...
PLAYING WITH MOOCH IS FUN — BUT AFTER...
I'M ALWAYS COVERED IN CAT FUR!

BONK
HEY! SHOULDN'T YOU BE STORING THESE FOR WINTER!?!
WHY DIDN'T WE THINK OF THAT !?!

NOW... NOW... HOLD STILL, EARL.
TA
DA!
WHAT DO YOU THINK?

IT MATCHES MY EYES.

EARL- DON'T YOU THINK THAT SHWEATER IS CHEATING?
CHEAT-ING!?! ON WHAT?!
EVOLUTION! IT'S SHURVIVAL OF THE "FITTEST" -NOT- OF THE "FITTED"!
HEY! WHERE CAN I GET ONE!?!

!
MY GOODNESS!
PUT ON SOME PANTS!

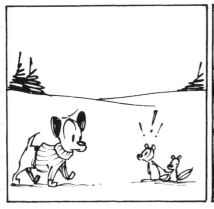

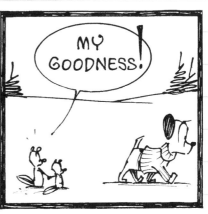

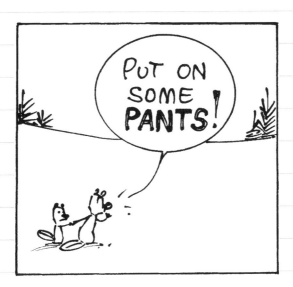

DANCES
WITH
SNOWFLAKES

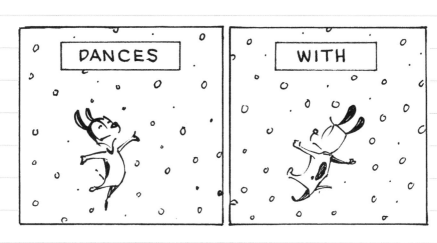

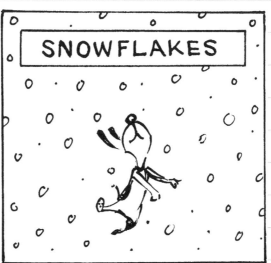

MOOCH, ARE YOU ALL SET TO HIBERNATE 'TIL SPRING?
ALL SET!
BLANKY...
PILLOW...
DING DONG
...PIZZA!

SORRY, EARL, MY HANDS ARE FULL.
HOWZABOUT A **FOOT** BELLY RUB?
RUB
RUB

BEGGARS SHOULD NOT BE CHOOSERS.

HOW AM I SUPPOSED TO EAT LOOKING AT THOSE EYES!?!
FLIP
FLOP

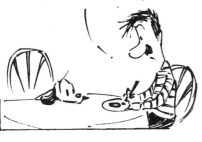

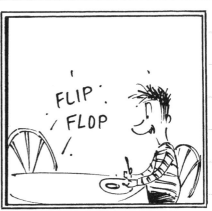

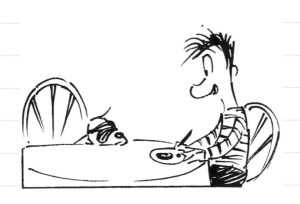

What makes Earl's tail wag?

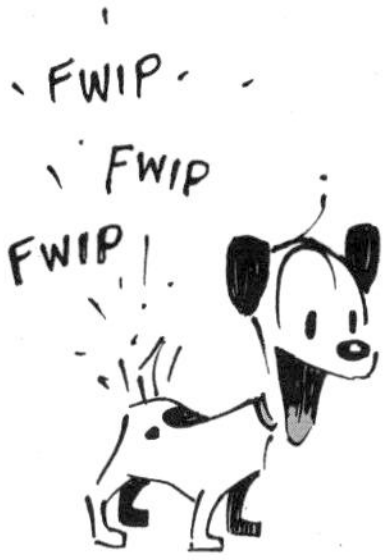
FWIP
FWIP
FWIP

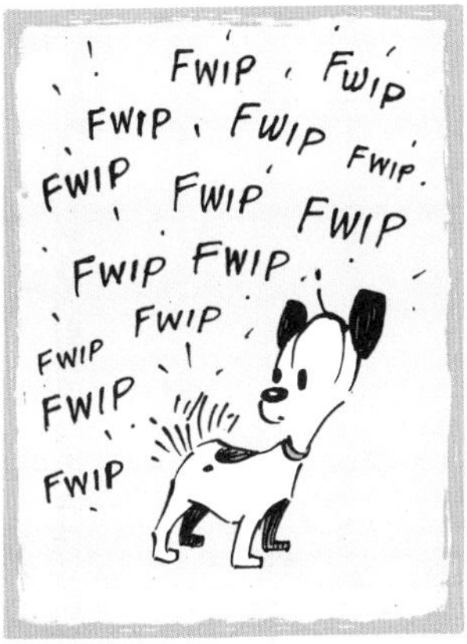
FWIP
FWIP
FWIP
FWIP
FWIP
FWIP
FWIP
FWIP
FWIP
FWIP
FWIP
FWIP
FWIP
FWIP

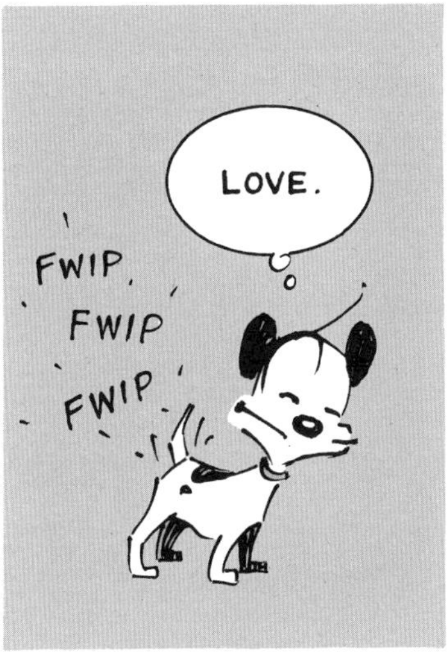
LOVE.
FWIP
FWIP
FWIP

THAT CAT
IS GETTING
TO ME.

Sour Puss' diary

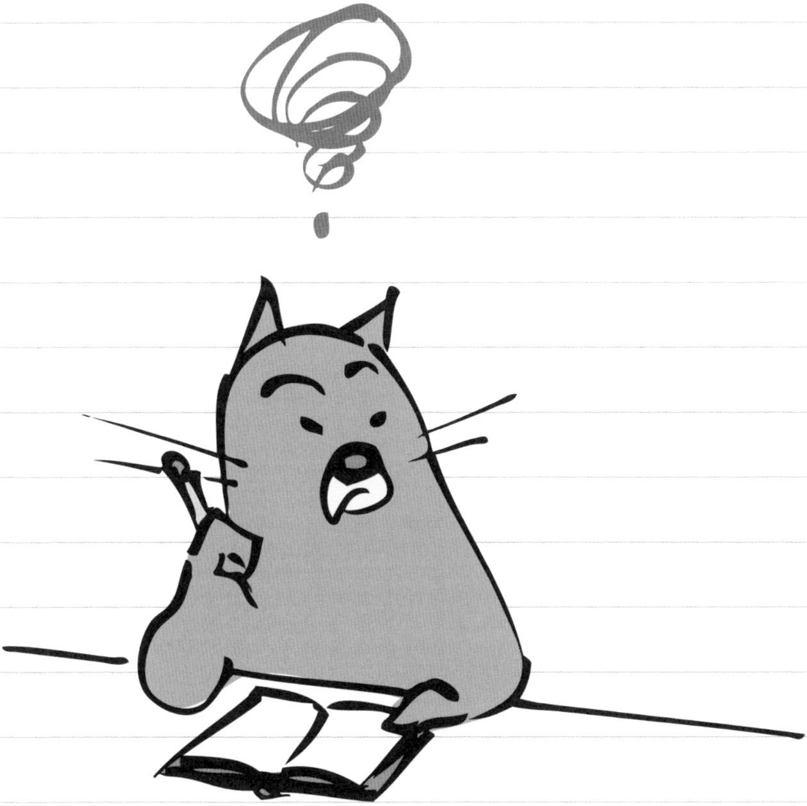

THIS IS MY
"LEAVE ME ALONE"
FACE
CAN'T
YOU READ!?!

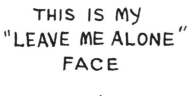

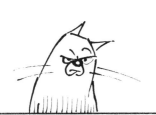

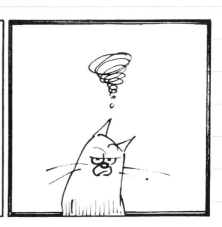

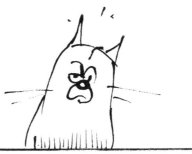

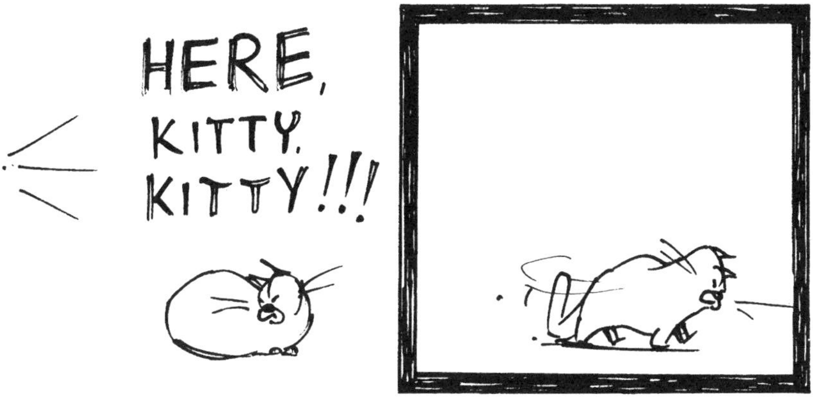
HERE,
KITTY,
KITTY!!!

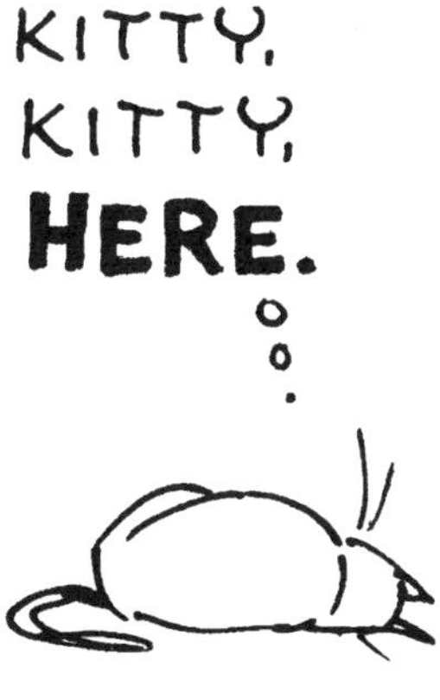
KITTY,
KITTY,
HERE.

I HATE MONDAYS.
BLAT
TODAY'S TUESDAY, "HAPPY-FACE"!
I MUST HAVE OVERSLEPT.

I HATE MONDAYS!
HATE 'EM!
HATE 'EM!
HATE 'EM!
CALM DOWN, SOURPUSS, —MARCH IS SUPPOSED TO GO OUT LIKE A **LAMB.**
BAH!

TODAY I DON'T WANT TO BE TOUCHED.
I DON'T EVEN WANT TO BE LOOKED AT!
TODAY AS FAR AS YOU'RE CONCERNED- **YOU** DON'T HAVE A KITTY!
I'LL BE HIDING UNDER THE SOFA-SO DON'T GO LOOKING FOR ME. JUST TRY TO **STAY OUT** OF MY LIFE. THANK YOU.
OH...
...I'LL HAVE FRESH TUNA AND WARM MILK FOR DIN-DIN.

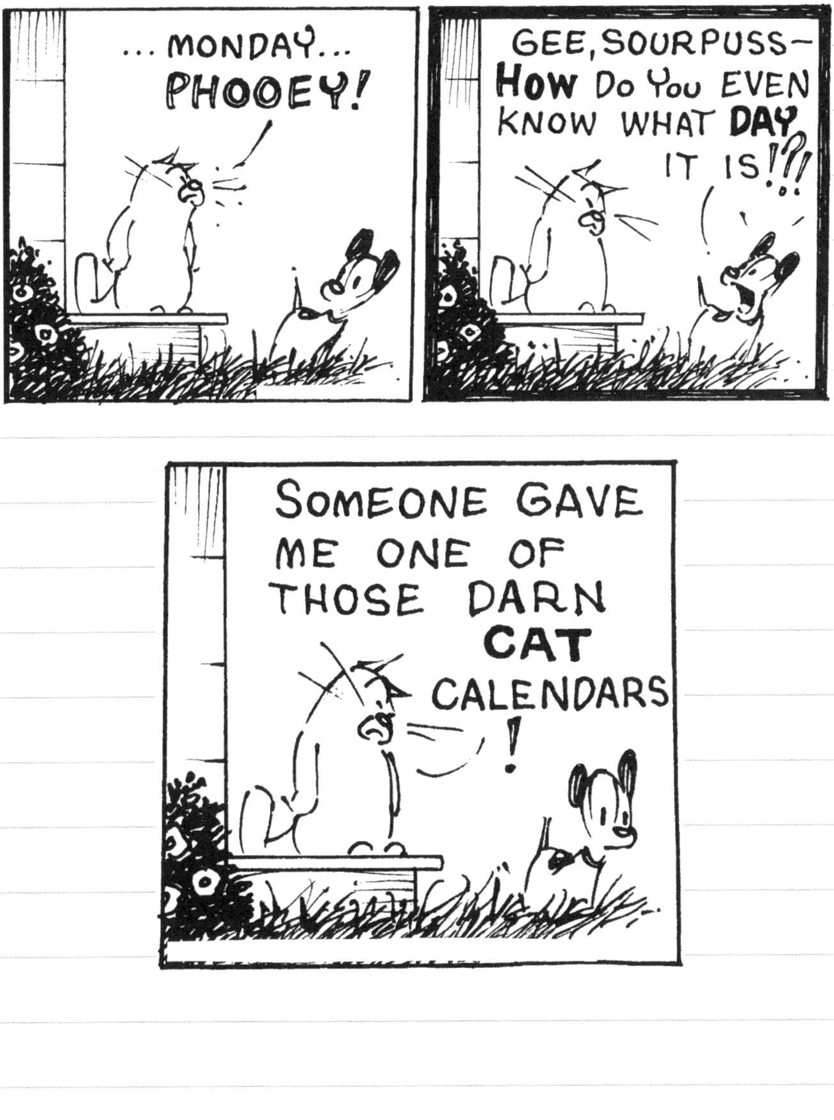

... MONDAY... PHOOEY!
GEE, SOURPUSS– HOW DO YOU EVEN KNOW WHAT DAY IT IS!?!
SOMEONE GAVE ME ONE OF THOSE DARN CAT CALENDARS!

LOOKS LIKE RAIN.
NO, IT DOESN'T!
BAH.
THAT LOOKS LIKE RAIN!

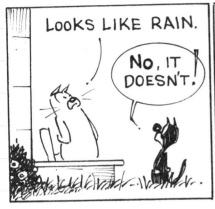

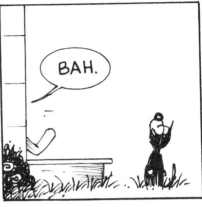

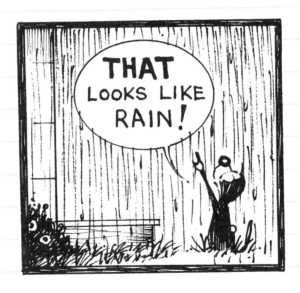

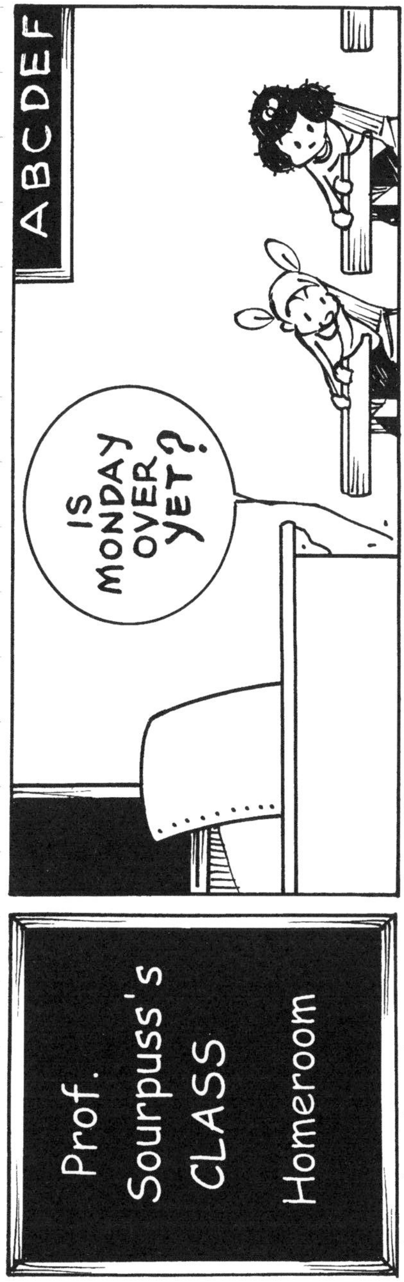
Prof. Sourpuss's CLASS Homeroom
ABCDEF
IS MONDAY OVER YET?

OH
WOE
OH
WOE
OH. WOE IS **ME**.
TOOT
PITY PARTY.

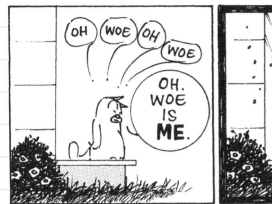

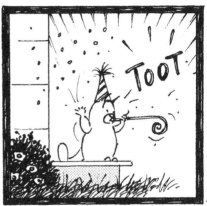

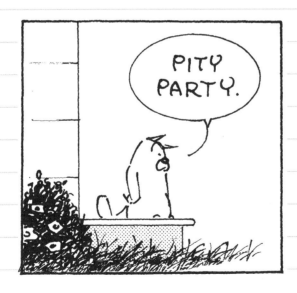

WHAT'S THE MATTER, SOURPUSS?
OH, EARL- NOTHING EVER SEEMS TO GO MY WAY.
BONK
THAT FIXES THAT.

I DON'T LIKE MONDAYS.
AND MONDAYS DON'T LIKE ME.

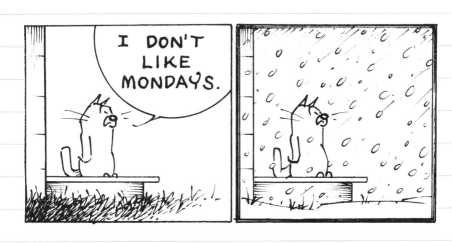

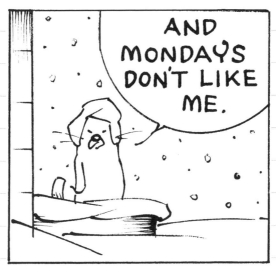

BAH.
DO YOU KNOW THE ONLY THING YOU'RE GOOD AT IS COMPLAINING?
YES.
PRACTICE MAKES PERFECT.

SOURPUSS' NEW YEAR'S RESOLUTIONS
1. SMILE
OKAY—
I CAN CROSS THAT ONE OFF.

CHicKpea's DiAry

SHELTER STORIES
CHICKPEA AND CHICKPEA'S BROTHER
I HOPE YOU FIND A HOME!
I HOPE YOU FIND A HOME!
HEY, MAYBE YOU'LL BE PICKED NEXT!
HEY, MAYBE YOU'LL BE PICKED NEXT!

WE'VE BEEN CAGED TOGETHER TOO LONG.
WE'VE BEEN CAGED TOGETHER TOO LONG.

SHELTER STORIES

CHICKPEA AND CHICKPEA'S BROTHER ©

THE PERSON WHO PICKS ME IS GOING TO GET KISSED AND LICKED LIKE THERE'S **No** TOMORROW!

THE PERSON WHO PICKS ME IS GOING TO GET PURRS AND CUDDLES **ALL** NIGHT LONG!

THE PERSON WHO PICKS ME.

SHELTER STORIES
CHICKPEA AND CHICKPEA'S BROTHER
I HOPE SOMEONE PICKS YOU TODAY!
I HOPE SOMEONE PICKS YOU TODAY!
I HOPE SOMEONE PICKS US TODAY!!!

A TWOFER!

SHELTER STORIES
CHICKPEA AND CHICKPEA'S BROTHER
HOW COME NOBODY EVER PICKS ME?
MAYBE THEY'RE LOOKING FOR SOMETHING DIFFERENT...
PICK ME.

SHELTER STORIES
CHICKPEA AND CHICKPEA'S BROTHER
WHAT HAPPENS IF NOBODY PICKS US?
NOBODY PICKS US!?! IMPOSSIBLE!
?
THE WORLD CAN'T BE THAT CRAZY!

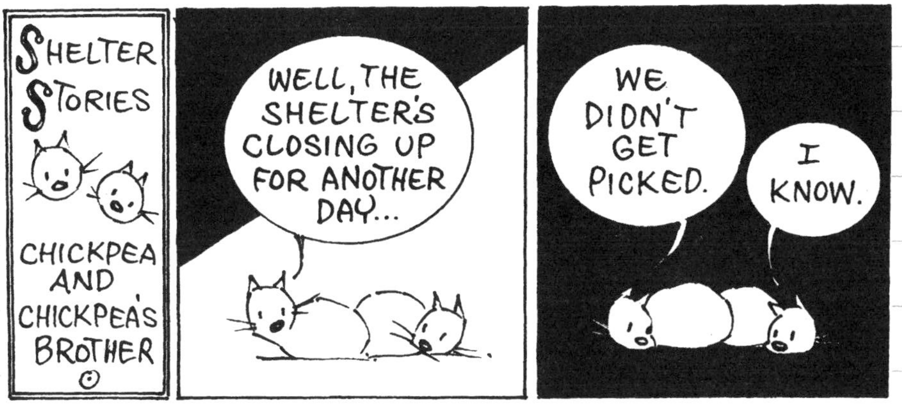
SHELTER STORIES
CHICKPEA AND CHICKPEA'S BROTHER
WELL, THE SHELTER'S CLOSING UP FOR ANOTHER DAY...
WE DIDN'T GET PICKED.
I KNOW.

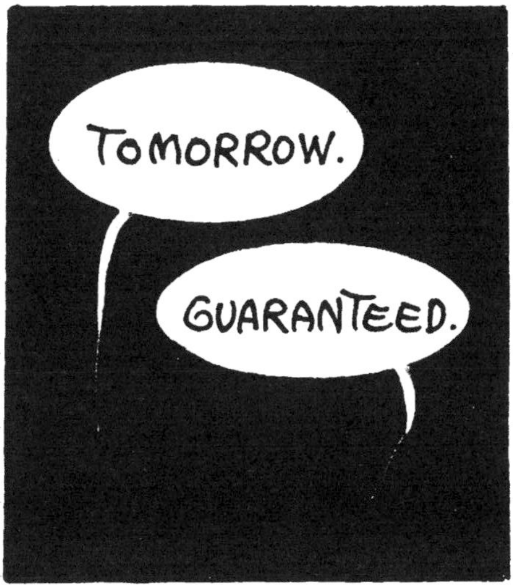
TOMORROW.
GUARANTEED.

SHELTER STORIES
CHICKPEA AND CHICKPEA'S BROTHER
I HOPE YOU GET ADOPTED TODAY!
I HOPE YOU GET ADOPTED TODAY!
GOOD LUCK!

SHELTER STORIES
CHICKPEA AND CHICKPEA'S BROTHER
I HOPE YOU GET ADOPTED!
I HOPE YOU GET ADOPTED!
I WON.

SHELTER STORIES
CHICKPEA AND CHICKPEA'S BROTHER.
CHICKPEA FINALLY GOT ADOPTED!
YAHOO!
HOW EXCITING! I CAN'T WAIT TO TELL...
... CHICKPEA...

SHELTER STORIES
CHICKPEA AND CHICKPEA'S BROTHER
CHICKPEA FINALLY GOT ADOPTED!
IT'S A DREAM COME TRUE. I COULDN'T BE HAPPIER!
SHNIFF

SHELTER STORIES

CHICKPEA AND CHICKPEA'S BROTHER

MY SIBLING CHICKPEA GOT ADOPTED!

WHAT COULD BE BETTER THAN **THAT!?!**

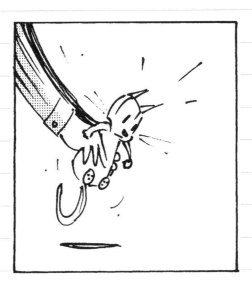

CHICKPEA AND CHICKPEA'S BROTHER, HOW DID YOU TWO LEAVE THE SHELTER?
EASY.
EVERY NIGHT I PRAYED YOU WOULD GET ADOPTED.
SOUNDS LIKE SOMEONE HEARD YOU.
IN STEREO

AS TWINS, SOMETIMES WE
FINISH EACH OTHERS SENTENCES
...AND SOMETIMES...
?

...NOT.
OH.

YIKES! HOW CAN YOU TELL EACH OTHER APART!?!
EASY.
THAT'S NOT ME.
I THINK.

CRabby's DiaRY

HEAT
SAND
SUN
HUMIDITY
CRAB SEASON.

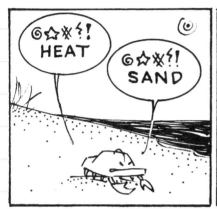

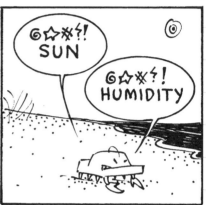

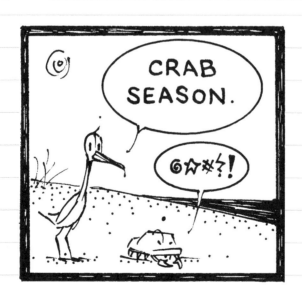

ENJOYING THE VIEW, CRABBY?
SURE
MY POINT OF VIEW.

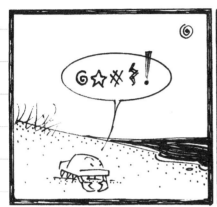

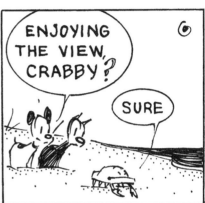

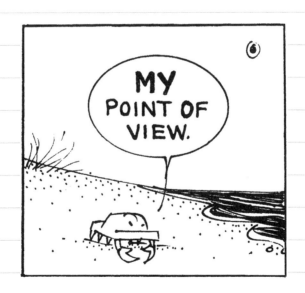

@☆※$! CLOUD.

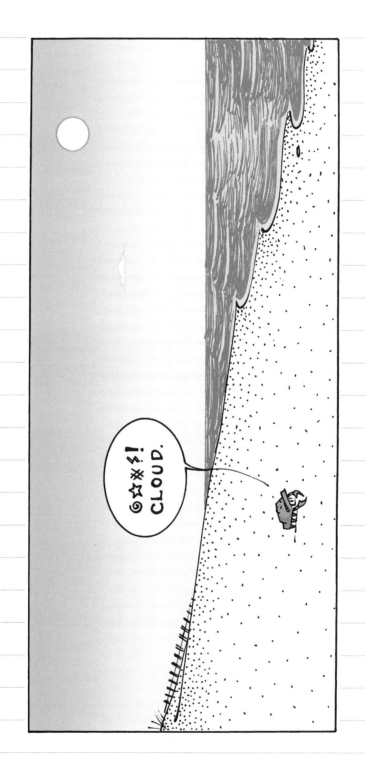

CRABBY—HERE'S A LIST OF WORDS YOU'RE **NOT** ALLOWED TO SAY!
WELL... WHAT DO YOU THINK?
I'M @☆*#! SPEECHLESS!

@☆*?!!
OOOOOH- I'M GOING TO TELL YOUR MOMMY WHAT YOU JUST SAID!!!
MRS. CRABBY?
MRS. CRABBY?
WHAT THE @☆#?! DO YOU WANT, YOUNG MAN?

OH, CRABBY — WHAT A **PERFECT** DAY! THERE'S ABSOLUTELY **NOTHING** TO COMPLAIN ABOUT.
YOU'RE RIGHT!

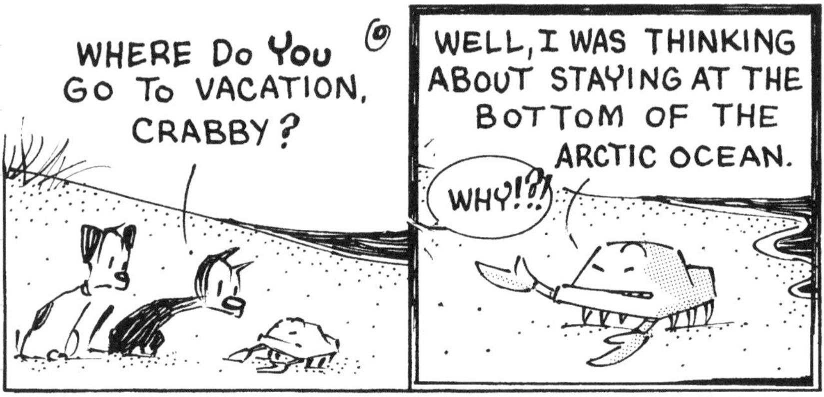
WHERE Do You GO To VACATION, CRABBY?
WELL, I WAS THINKING ABOUT STAYING AT THE BOTTOM OF THE ARCTIC OCEAN.
WHY!?!

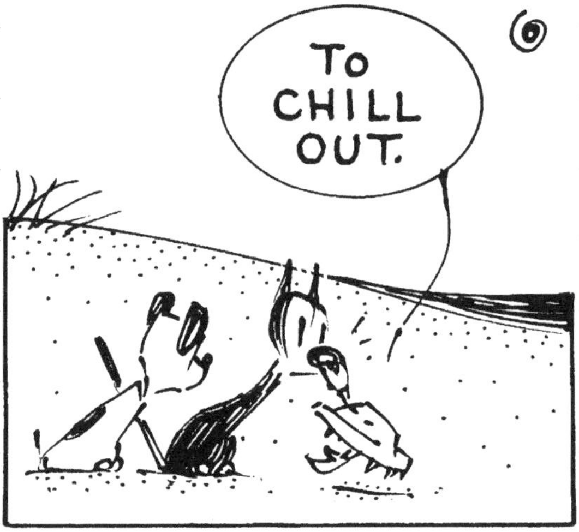
To CHILL OUT.

UMF...THAT'S NOT WHAT I MEANT...
...WHEN I SAID "LET'S DO LUNCH"!

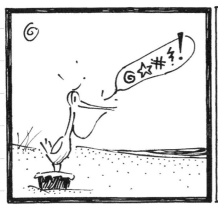

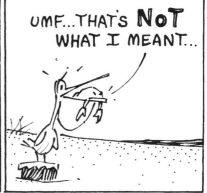

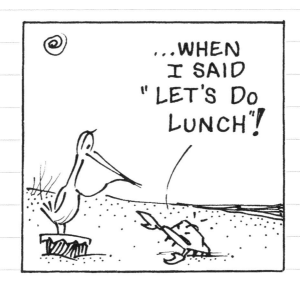

I'M THE BRAINS OF THIS OUTFIT.
AND WHAT'S HE?
HE'S THE MUSSEL.

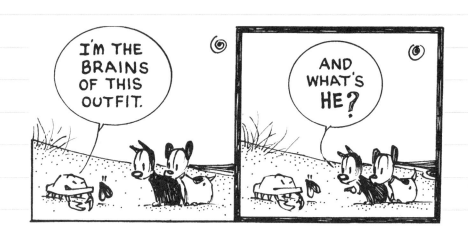

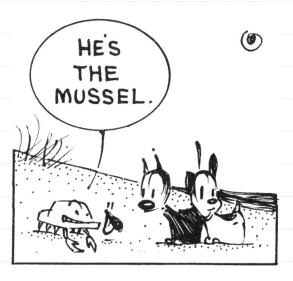

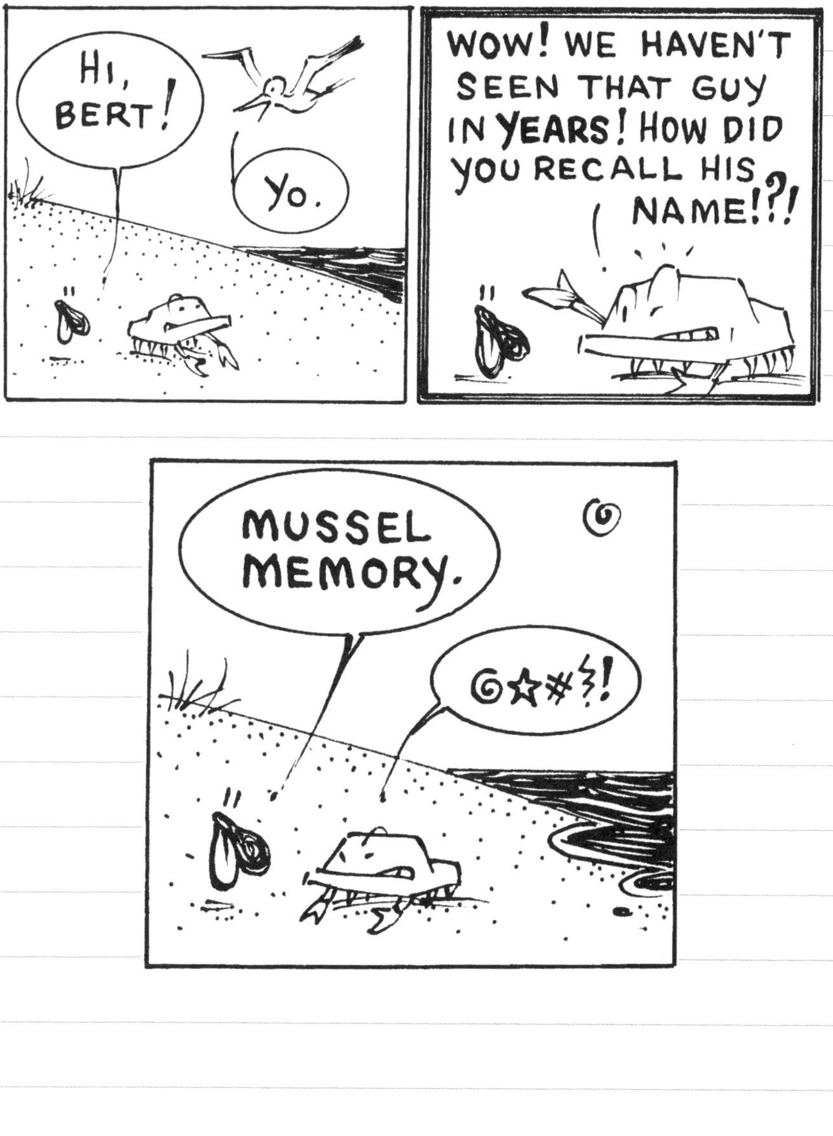
HI, BERT!
YO.
WOW! WE HAVEN'T SEEN THAT GUY IN YEARS! HOW DID YOU RECALL HIS NAME!?!
MUSSEL MEMORY.

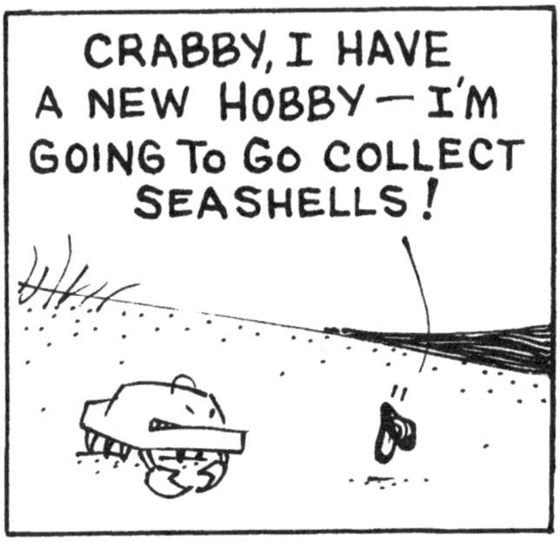
CRABBY, I HAVE A NEW HOBBY — I'M GOING TO GO COLLECT SEASHELLS!

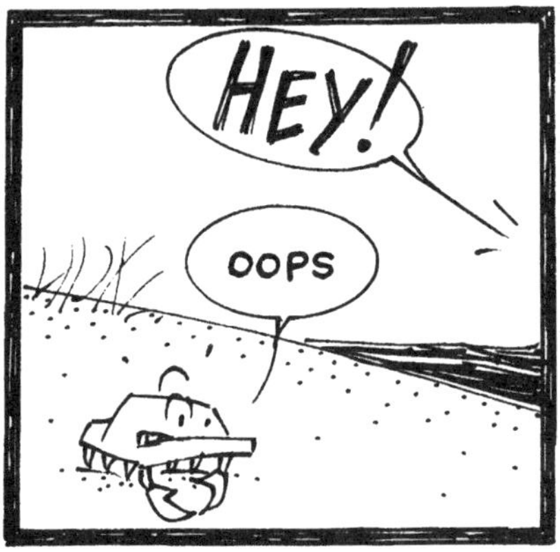
HEY!
OOPS

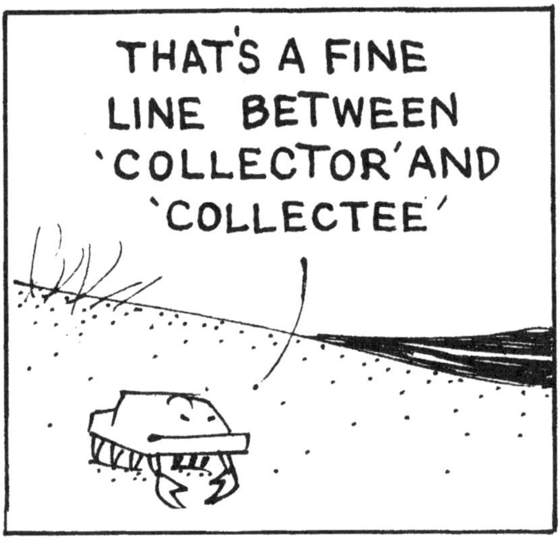
THAT'S A FINE LINE BETWEEN 'COLLECTOR' AND 'COLLECTEE'

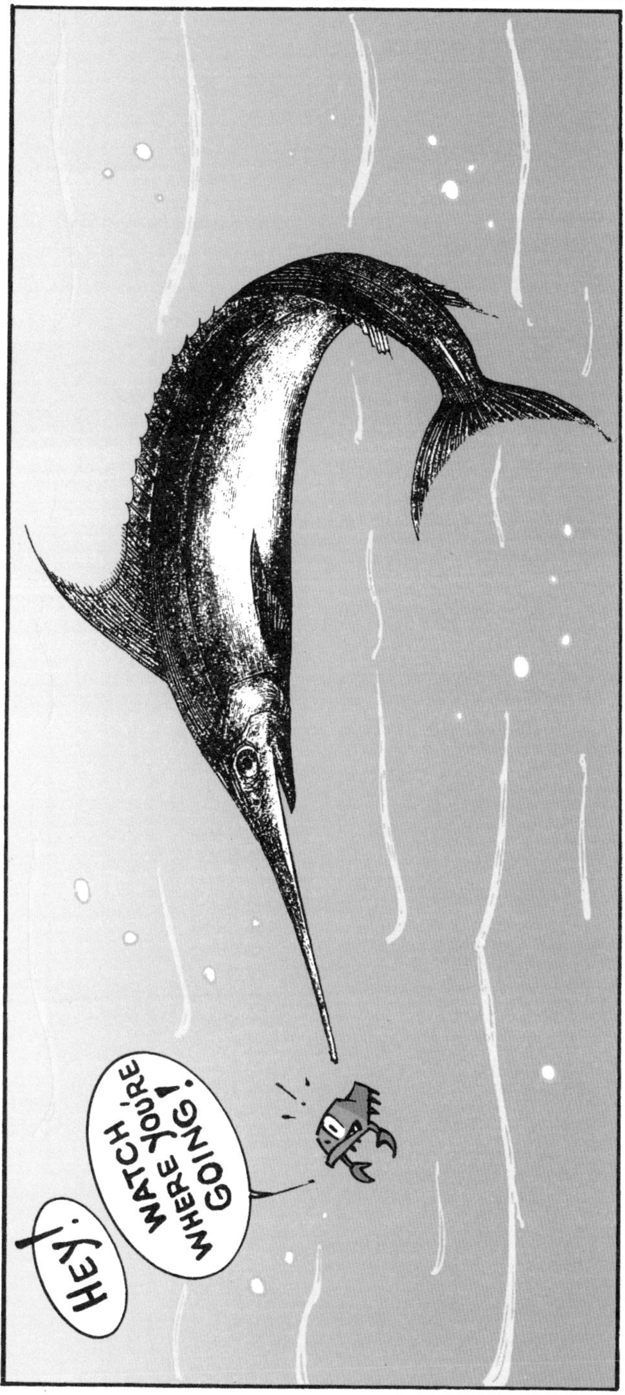
HEY!
WATCH WHERE YOU'RE GOING!

I LOVE THE ROAR OF THE OCEAN.
MY.
IT'S EXTRA ROUGH TODAY

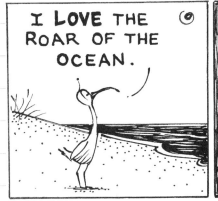

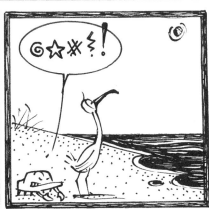

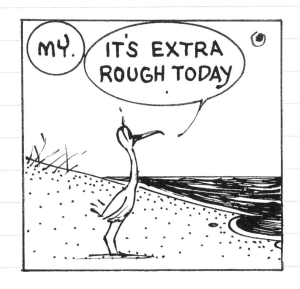

HEY, McGARRY- WHERE'S THAT @☆#⚡! CAT AND @☆#⚡! DOG!?!
THEY WENT HOME.
GEE, DO YOU @☆#⚡! THINK IT WAS @☆#⚡! SOMETHING I @☆#⚡! SAID!?!
YOU?!
ONLY EVERY OTHER WORD!
I WONDER WHAT THE @☆#⚡! IT WAS!?!

I THINK I LEFT ONE OF MY LI'L PINK SOCKS AT THE BEACH!
PINK SOCK
PINK SOCK

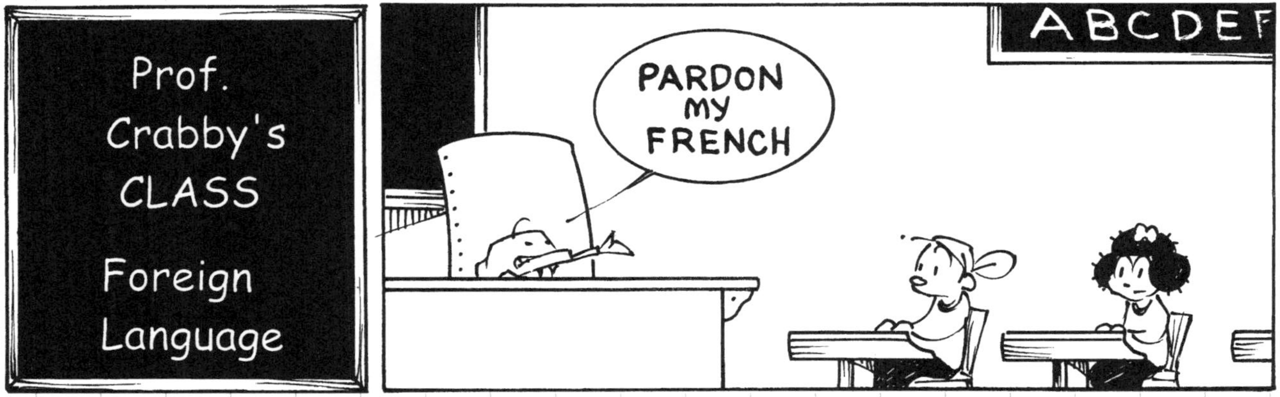
Prof. Crabby's CLASS
Foreign Language
ABCDEF
PARDON MY FRENCH

ARG!
@☆#$!
I'M SICK OF IT! WHAT A @☆#$! MESS! ENOUGH ALREADY!
SNOW CRAB.

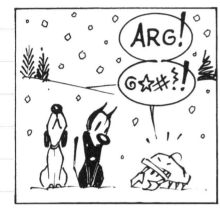

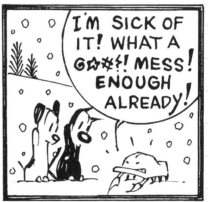

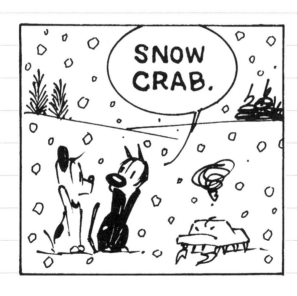

Guard Dog's Diary

BARK
BARK
BARK
BARK
I BARK
THEREFORE I AM.

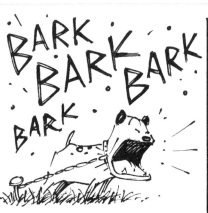

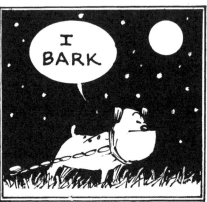

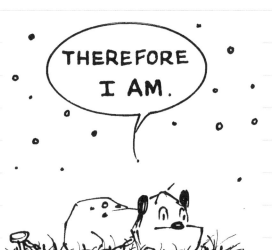

I START EVERY DAY BELIEVING TODAY IS THE DAY I'LL BE UNCHAINED.
OH... BEAUTIFUL DAY.

OH, YOU POOR, POOR THING. TIED UP IN CHAINS ALL DAY.
WOULD YOU LIKE SOME OF MY SCHOOL LUNCH?
I'M IN LOVE.

OH, HERE COMES THAT GIRL WHO TREATS ME SO KINDLY.
WAG
WAG WAG
OH
MY.
I THOUGHT I FORGOT HOW TO DO THAT.

HOW ARE YOU DOING TODAY, PAL? I MADE YOU SOME TREATS
DOG BONES!
SORRY, I HAD MORE—BUT I GOT HUNGRY IN MATH CLASS.

TIED UP ALL THE TIME AND YOU ARE STILL A **SWEETIE** – I DON'T KNOW HOW YOU DO IT!
THE CHAINS AROUND MY NECK
NOT MY HEART.

OKAY, PAL, I HAVE TO GO TO SCHOOL NOW ~ BUT I HOPE TO SEE YOU SOON.
DON'T WORRY
I'LL BE HERE.

GEE... I'M NOT MUCH OF A WATCHDOG ANYMORE...
NOW I'M JUST WATCHING TIME GO BY...
UNTIL THAT SWEET GIRL COMES BACK.

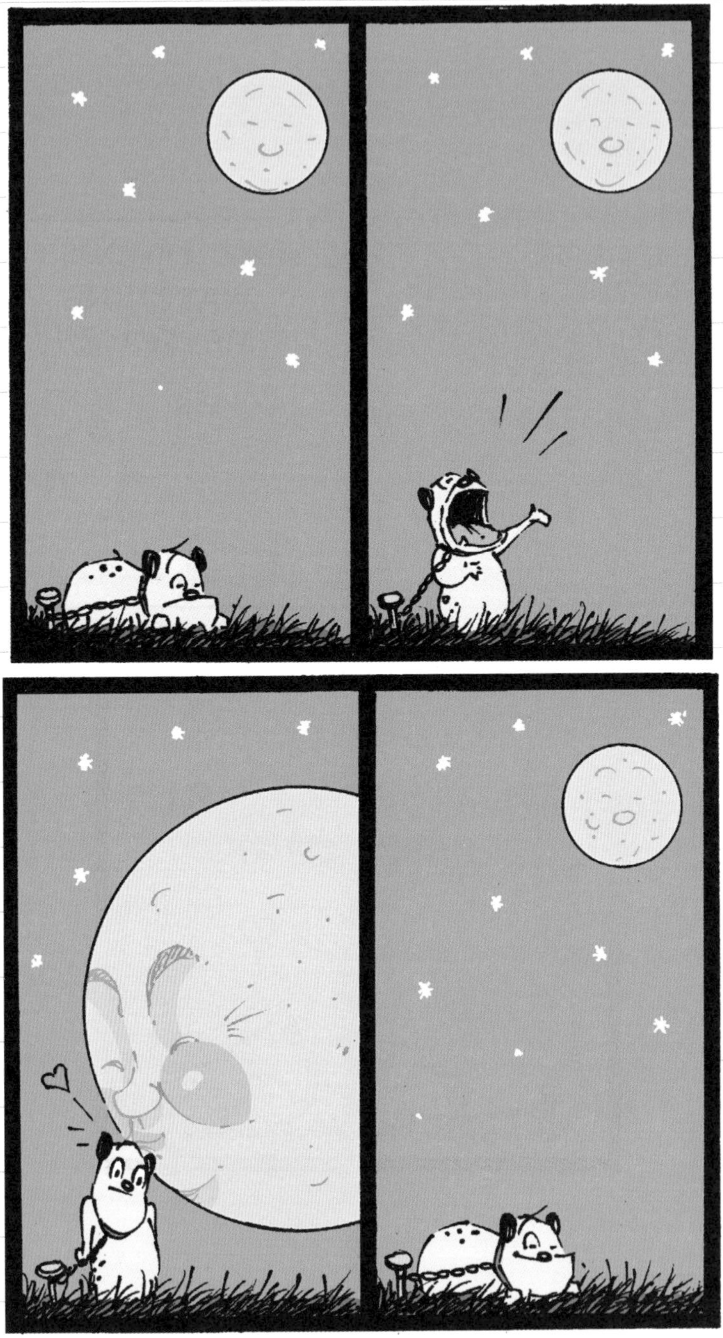

HEY, GUARD DOG, DID YOU GET A CHANCE TO VACATION ANY-WHERE THIS SUMMER
?
No.
I WAS A LITTLE TIED UP.

MAYBE I DON'T WANT A GIFT FROM **YOUR** VACATION! YOU KNOW— SOME OF US **NEVER** GO ON VACATION!!!
IF YOU PUT IT TO YOUR **EAR** YOU CAN HEAR THE **OCEAN**.

AUGH... MOOCH, I ATE SOMETHING THAT DISAGREED WITH ME...
GURGLE
WEE OOOOG
GURGLE
SOUNDS LIKE IT'S SHTILL COMPLAINING

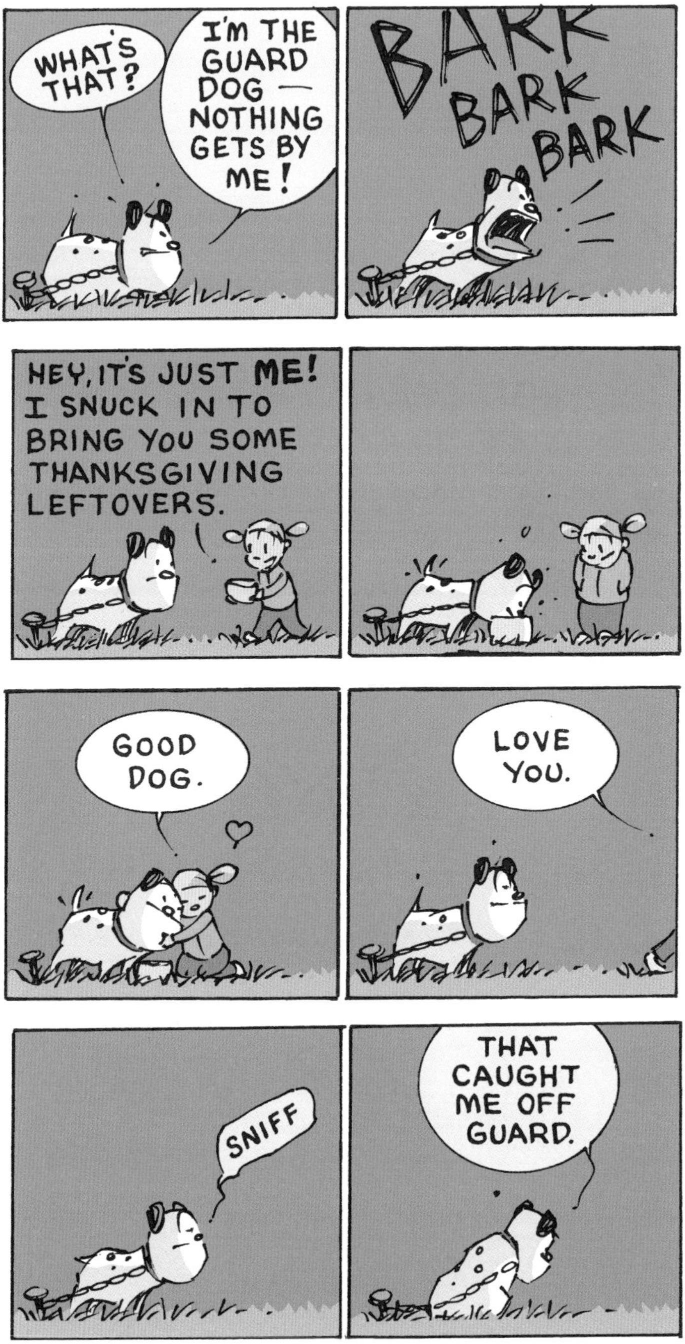
WHAT'S THAT?
I'M THE GUARD DOG — NOTHING GETS BY ME!
BARK
BARK
BARK
HEY, IT'S JUST ME! I SNUCK IN TO BRING YOU SOME THANKSGIVING LEFTOVERS.
GOOD DOG.
LOVE YOU.
SNIFF
THAT CAUGHT ME OFF GUARD.

BARK
BARK
BARK
BARK
BARK
BA
BARK
QUIET!
THERE'S SO MUCH I WANTED TO SAY.

Bip and Bop's diary

I'M OBSESSED WITH THROWING ACORNS —I THINK I NEED HELP!
BONK
YOU SHOULD PUT MORE WEIGHT ON YOUR BACK FOOT.

BONK
WHAT HAPPENED?
I WAS ASSAULTED WITH A PEANUT!
ACTUALLY, THAT WAS UNSALTED.

BONK
DON'T YOU HAVE ANYTHING BETTER TO DO?
BETTER THAN THIS!?!

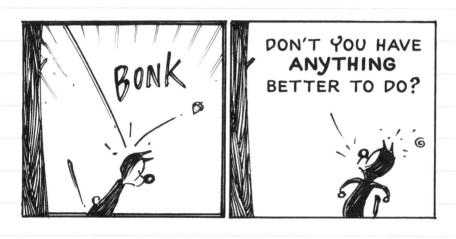

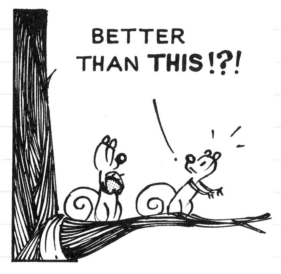

NO MORE BONKING HEADS! I'M DONE WITH ACORNS!
BONK
JUST WHEN I THOUGHT I WAS OUT-THEY PULL ME BACK IN!!!

BONK
HEY!
YOU SHOULD SEE A PSYCHIATRIST!
NO-YOU SHOULD SEE
A PSYCHI-ATRIST!
I'M NOT ALLOWED ON THE COUCH.

WHAT'S THAT, BIP?
A CASHEW!
GESUNDHEIT.

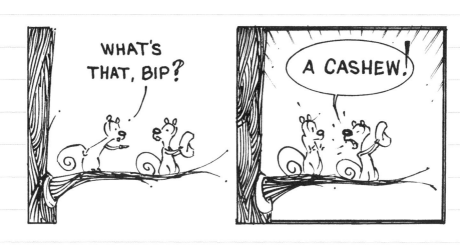

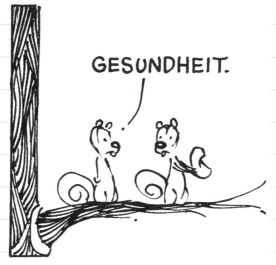

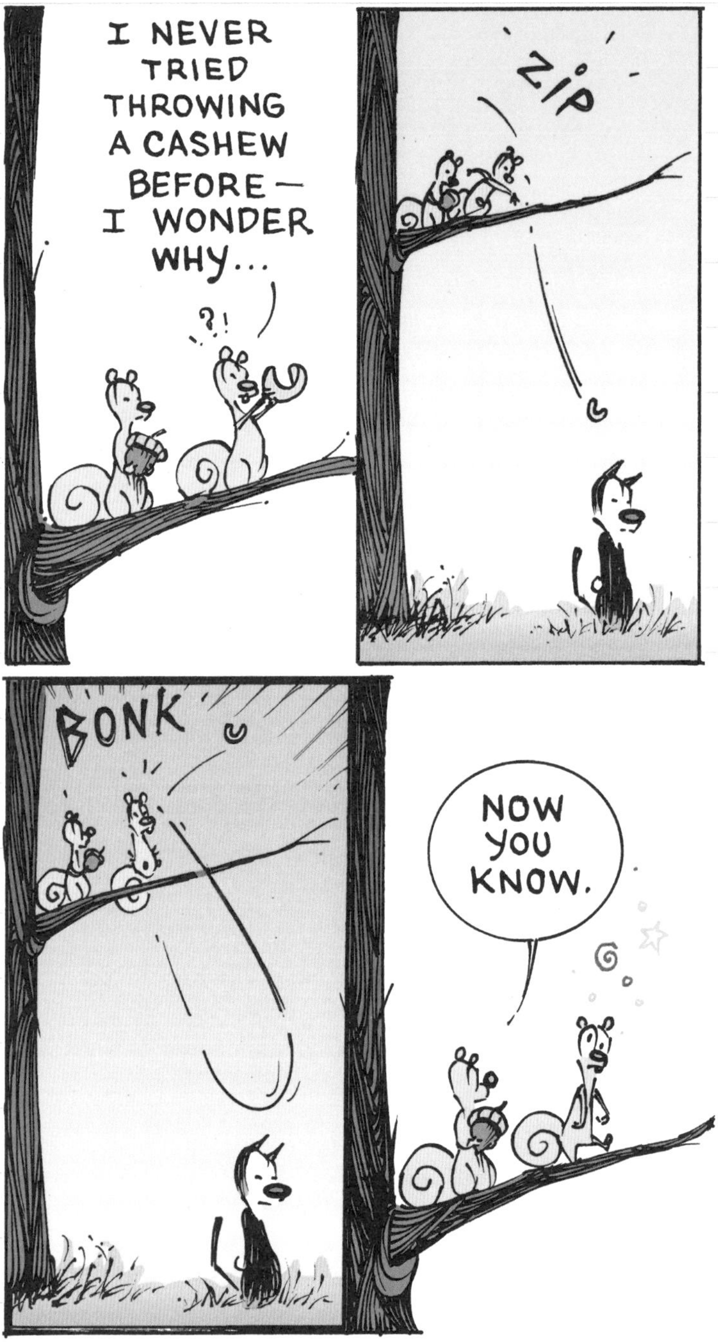
I NEVER TRIED THROWING A CASHEW BEFORE—I WONDER WHY...
?!
ZIP
BONK
NOW YOU KNOW.

BOP
THE FIRST DAY OF SUMMER.

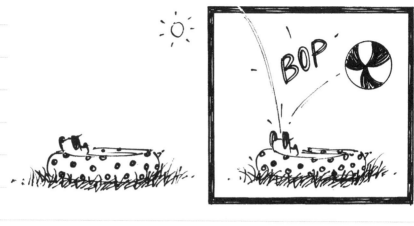

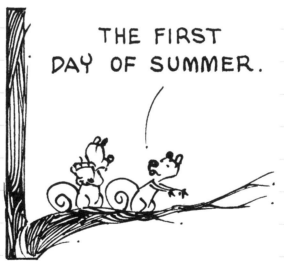

LAP
LICK
LAP
HEY! THIS IS A WADING POOL!!!
OH
I THOUGHT IT WAS 'DOG SOUP.'

A BARBECUE IS FUN!
YESH!
BONK
BUT IT AIN'T NO PICNIC.

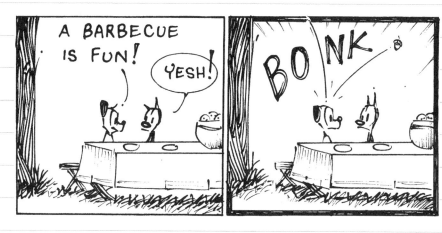

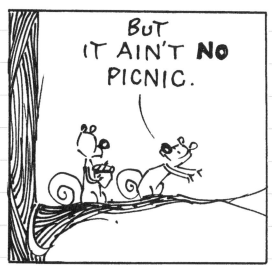

KLANG
THAT SHOULD KNOCK THE RUST OFF.

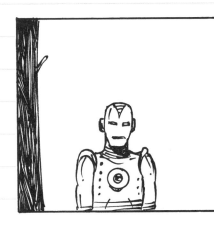

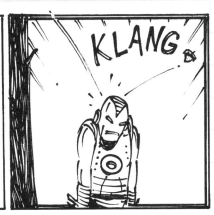

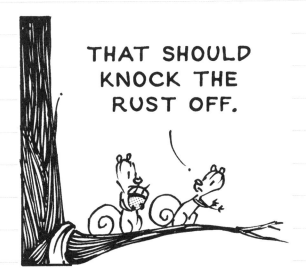

BONK
THAT SHOULD KNOCK SOME SPIDEY SENSE INTO HIM.

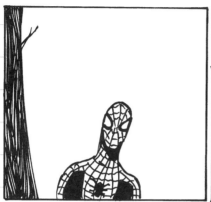

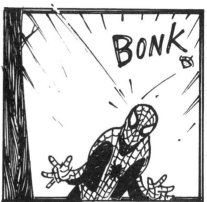

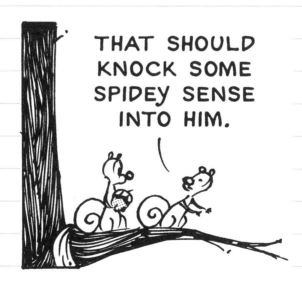

EGADS!
YOUR HOME IS FILLED WITH NUTS!
SIGH...
I HAVE TO ADMIT...
I'M A HOARDER.

YOU CAN'T HOARD EVERYTHING!!! HERE—TRY THROWING THIS ACORN AWAY!
BONK
NOW-DID THAT HURT?
YESH!

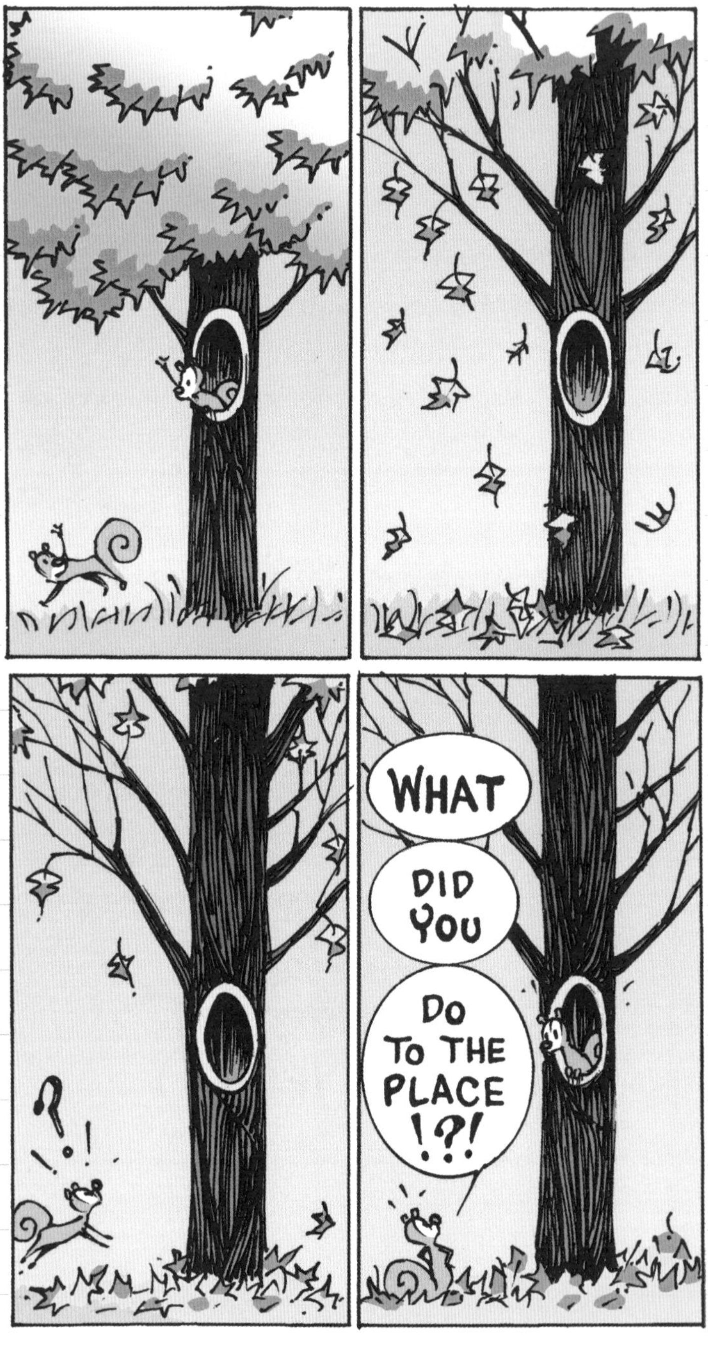
WHAT
DID YOU
DO TO THE PLACE !?!

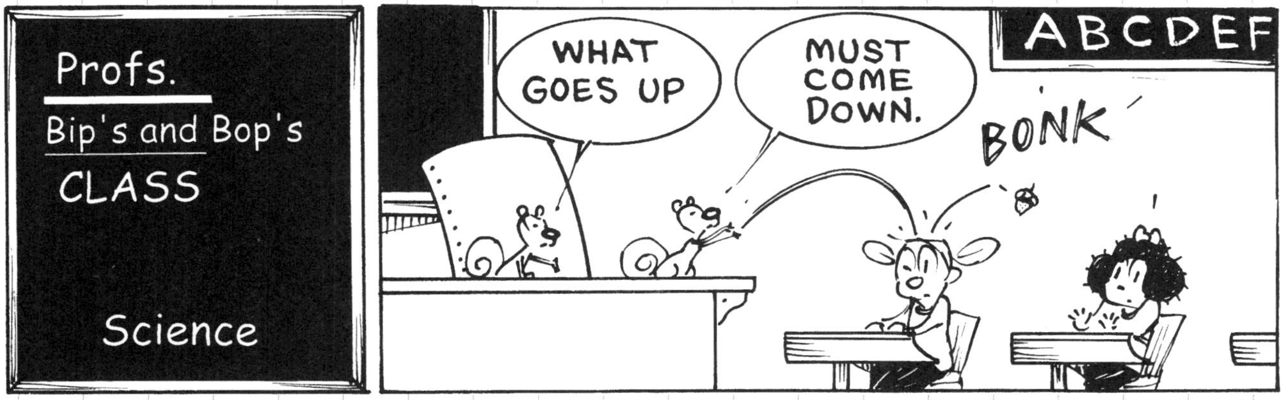
Profs.
Bip's and Bop's
CLASS
Science
ABCDEF
WHAT GOES UP
MUST COME DOWN.
BONK

BONK
THIS IS A NO-SMOKING ZONE.

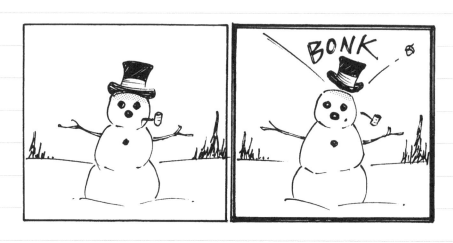

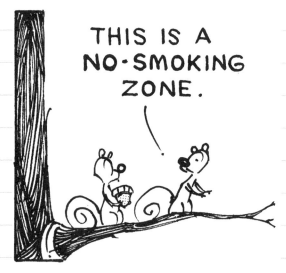

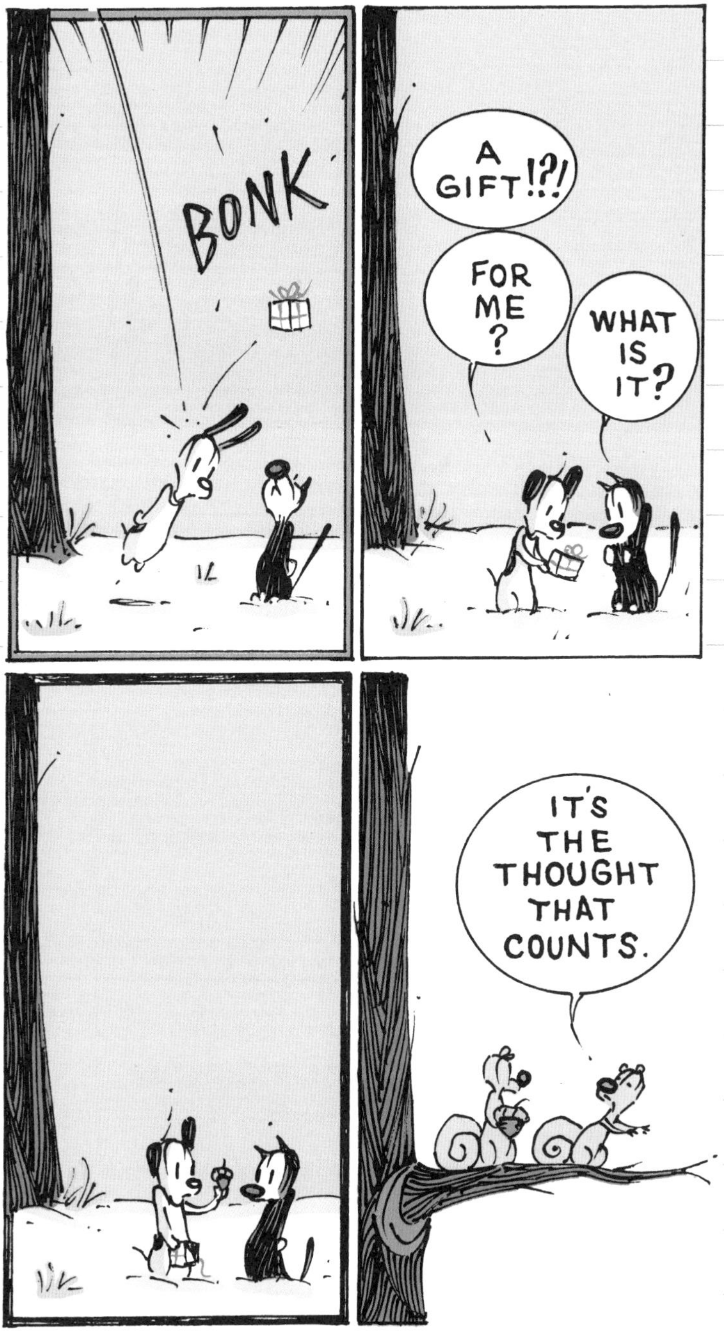
BONK
A GIFT!?!
FOR ME?
WHAT IS IT?
IT'S THE THOUGHT THAT COUNTS.

BONK

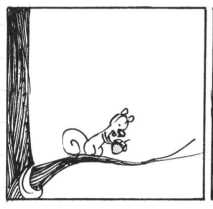

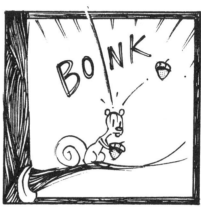

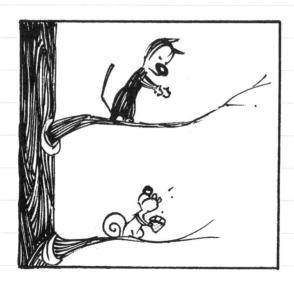

SHtiNKY's DiaPy

SHTINKY'S
TO·DO LIST
1. SAVE THE WORLD.
WOW
IT'S A GOOD THING I GOT UP EARLY.

I'VE DECIDED INSTEAD OF TRYING TO FIGHT ALL THE ILLS OF THE WORLD I WOULD JUST LOVE AND HUG EVERYTHING.
HOW RIDICULOUS! HOW NAIVE!!! HOW
...ABOUT THAT!?!

YOU LOOK LIKE YOU COULD USE A HUG.
I DO!?!
I DID.

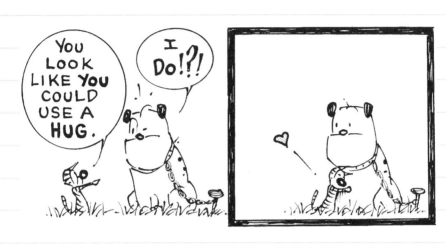

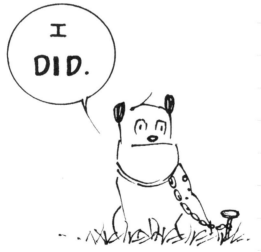

I DON'T KNOW MY OWN STRENGTH.

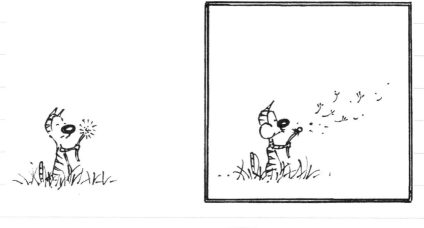

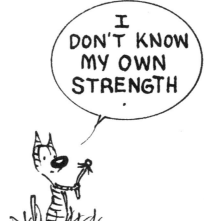

SAVE the TIGER
SAVE the TIGER
GOOD LUCK.
THANKS
BELIEVE!
SAVE the TIGER

SHTINKY, WITH YOUR ORANGE SHTRIPES—
DO YOU THINK YOU HAVE 'TIGER' IN YOUR BLOOD?
WELL
I KNOW THEY'RE IN MY HEART.

Shtinky's Animal Sanctuary • ALL • Welcome
Shtinky's Animal Sanctuary • ALL • Welcome
...SIGH...
Shtink Animal Sanctuary • ALL • Welcome
MAYBE TIGERS CAN'T READ.

IT'S **SO** WARM AND SAFE UNDER THE COVERS.
I WISH I COULD FIT THE **WHOLE** WORLD IN HERE.

SHTINKY-I KNOW THE WORLD CAN SEEM CRUEL AND UNFAIR, BUT WE CAN'T JUST HIDE UNDER THE COVERS!
YOU CAN MAKE A DIFFERENCE-GET OUT THERE-SPREAD THE LOVE AND HELP CHANGE THE WORLD!
I KNOW.

CAN I BRING MY BLANKY?

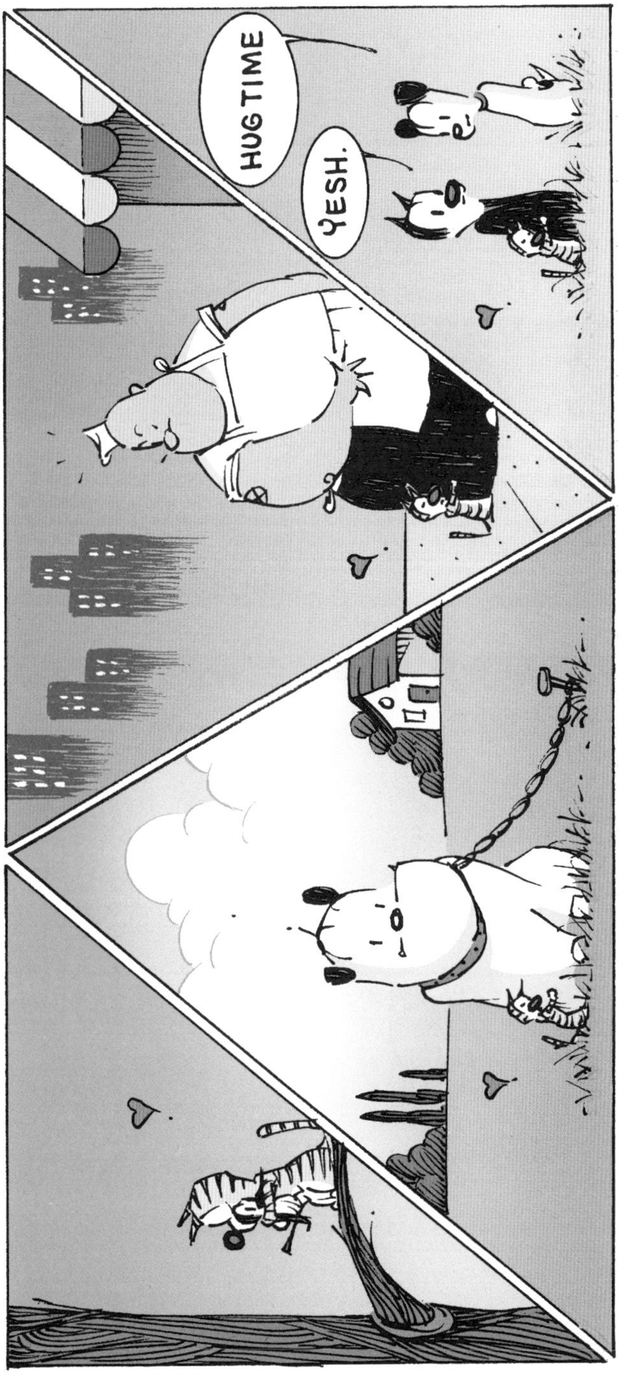
HUG TIME
YESH.

WHAT ARE YOU DOING, SHTINKY ?
WAITING
WAITING FOR WHAT !?!
THE RAIN TO STOP.

?
SHTINKY, ARE YOU LOST?
WELL...
I KNOW THAT I'M HERE.
I JUST DON'T KNOW
WHERE "HERE" IS.

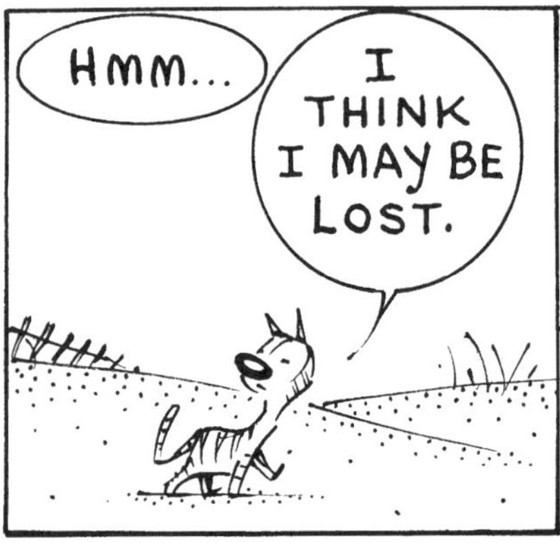
HMM...
I THINK I MAY BE LOST.

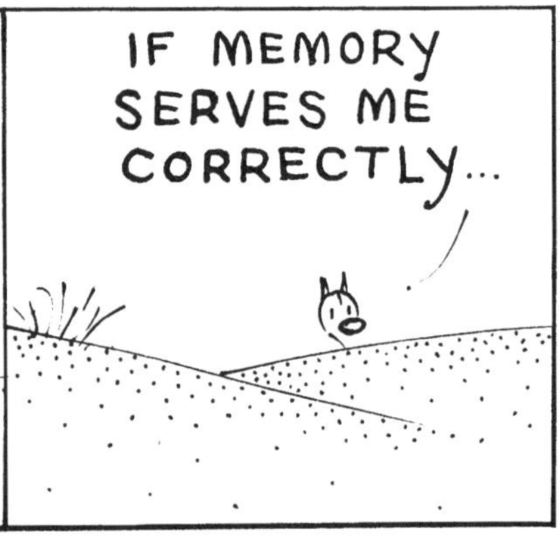
IF MEMORY SERVES ME CORRECTLY...

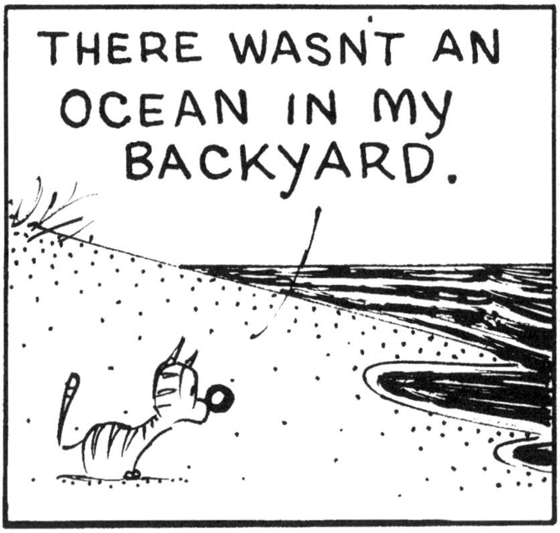
THERE WASN'T AN OCEAN IN MY BACKYARD.

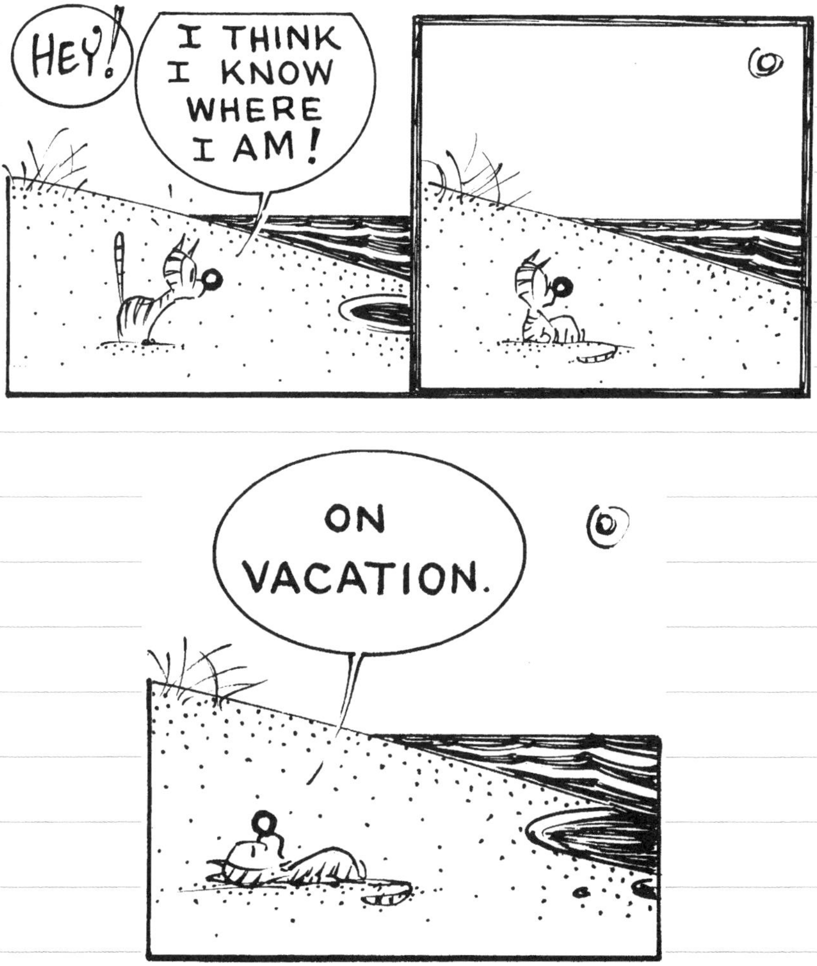
HEY!
I THINK I KNOW WHERE I AM!
ON VACATION.

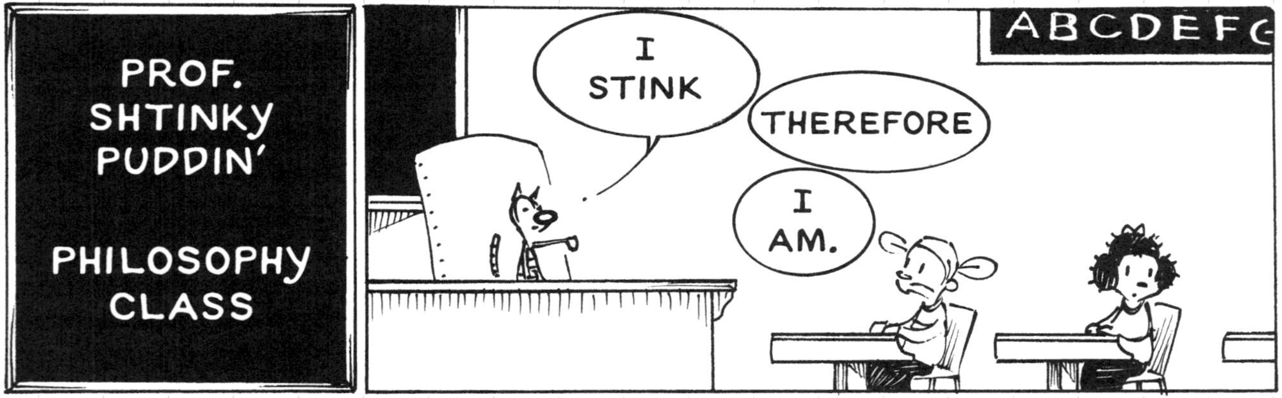
PROF.
SHTINKY
PUDDIN'
PHILOSOPHY
CLASS
ABCDEFG
I STINK
THEREFORE
I AM.

OOO!
HUG A TREE!
I THINK I BROKE IT.

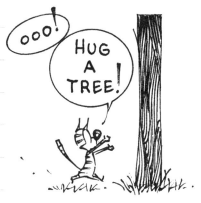

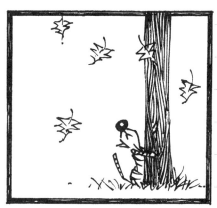

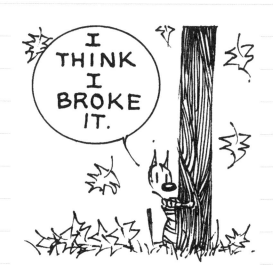

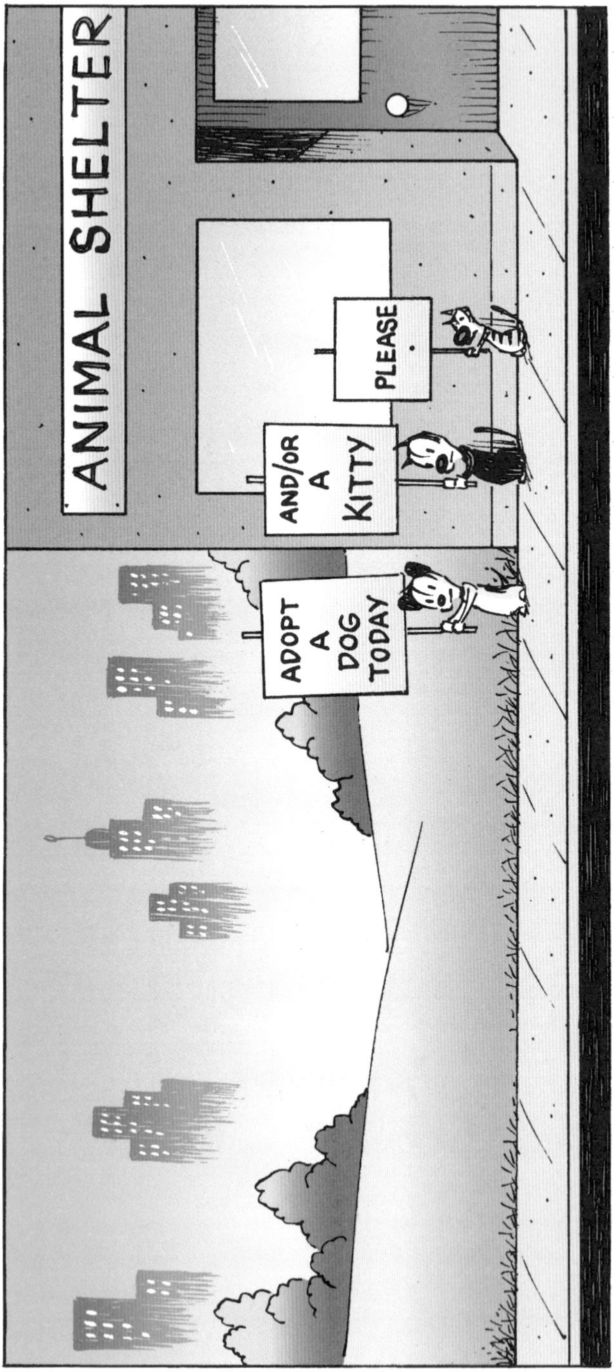
ANIMAL SHELTER
ADOPT A DOG TODAY
AND/OR A KITTY
PLEASE

Mutts is distributed internationally by King Features Syndicate, Inc. For information, write to King Features Syndicate, Inc., 300 West Fifty-Seventh Street, New York, New York 10019, or visit www.KingFeatures.com.

Andrews McMeel Publishing, LLC
an Andrews McMeel Universal company
1130 Walnut Street, Kansas City, Missouri 64106

15 16 17 18 19 SDB 11 10 9 8 7 6 5 4 3 2

ISBN: 978-1-4494-5870-6

Library of Congress Control Number: 2014931551

Printed on recycled paper.

Mutts can be found on the Internet at www.muttscomics.com

Cover design by Jeff Schulz

Made by:
Shenzhen Donnelley Printing Company Ltd.
Address and location of manufacturer:
No. 47, Wuhe Nan Road, Bantian Ind. Zone,
Shenzhen China, 518129
2nd Printing — 3/16/15

Check out these and other books at ampkids.com

 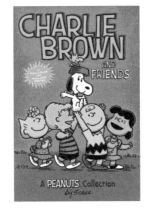 

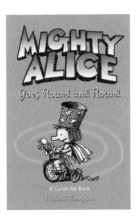 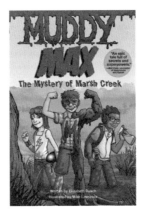 

Also available:
Teaching and activity guides for each title.
AMP! Comics for Kids books make reading FUN!